Fin, F...

Three o...

Sugarhouse Press

Sugarhouse Press
Freetown, Massachusetts
"Putting local pen to global paper"
www.sugarhousepress.com

This book is offered for sale at the price quoted only on the understanding that if any additional copies of the whole or any part are necessary for its production, such additional copies will be purchased. The attention of all purchasers is directed to the fact that this work is protected under the copyright laws of the United States of America, in the British Empire, including the Dominion of Canada, and all other countries adhering to the Universal Copyright Convention. Violations of the Copyright Law are punishable by fine and imprisonment, or both. The copying or duplication of this work or any part of this work by hand or any process, is an infringement of the copyright will be vigorously prosecuted. The holder of the rights to this piece uses the internet to protect against unauthorized production of his work.

Each of these plays may be produced by schools and amateurs for $50 for the first performance, and $25 for each subsequent performance, regardless of whether they are performed individually, or together in any combination. The cost for professionals is $100/play, each performance. To apply for rights, submit application to the publisher: Sugarhouse Press, 2 Washburn Rd., East Freetown, MA 02717, or email dbliss@sugarhousepress.com. Applications must include the name, address, email and phone number of the company; the number and dates of all performances. Royalties are due from all performances under any circumstances of production. Professional rights, reading rights, radio broadcasting, television and all mechanical rights are strictly reserved. Payment is expected at least one month prior to the first performance by check made out to "Don Bliss."

Copyright ©2018, Don Bliss and Sugarhouse Press

All rights reserved.

Printed in the U.S.A.

ISBN 978-1-387-49135-3

Important Note

All producers of "*Five Easy Pisces*, *The Cattish Play*, and *Fowl Play*" shall credit Don Bliss as the original author of this work on all programs, posters, webpages and other printed matter such as paid advertising under the producer's control. The credit to the author shall be not less than fifty percent (50%) of the size of type used for the title of the play. Said billing shall appear on a separate line following the title of the play and shall appear in the following form:

"[*Name of Producer*]

presents

[*the name of the play*]

by Don Bliss"

Five Easy Pisces

A Play Within a Play Within a Fish Tank.

The lobby aquarium of the Sculch Cove Playhouse. The fish, taking their responsibilities as entertainers very seriously, are working through the usual challenges of mounting a production of "Othello" on a very limited budget, amidst the intrigues of theater life and complicated "interpiscene" relationships. In a world where the big fish eat the little fish, the lives of these piscine actors reflect the themes of the very play they are producing for the mostly unnoticing patrons of the Sculch Cove Playhouse. Their world and their play revolve around trust and distrust.

Dramatis Piscae:

ROBERT WHITECHEEK-TANG, a White Cheek Tang, the Director

RAYETTE RADIATA, a Lionfish, the lead actress

ELTON, a Clownfish, the Stage Manager

STONEY, a Cubicus Boxfish, an actor

TWINKY, a Moorish Idolfish, the leading actor

LORNA, a Threadfin Butterflyfish an actress, and Rayette's friend

PARTITA AUREUS, a Golden Damselfish, Twinky's "friend"

PAT PUFFERFISH, a Pufferfish, the company Manager

KIMMY ECHINASTER, a Starfish, an actress

YELLOW TANGS, stage fins

ROYAL GRAMMA BASSLETS, dancers, actors,

The following music is referenced in the script. Rights for these pieces must be arranged separately. *'One/Reprise'* by Marvin Hamlisch and Edward Lawrence Kleban, © Sony/ATV Harmony; *'Tossin' and Turnin''* by Bobby Lewis, © EMI, Blackwood Music Inc.; *'Lady Marmalade'* by Bob Crewe, ©EMI/Jobete Music Co. Inc.; *'That's Amore'* by Jack Brooks and Harry Warren, © Four Jays Music Co..

The set: The entire play takes place in the aquarium. Actors never actually leave the stage, but are continually swimming somewhere within sight of the audience. All actors dress in black, with full head hoods. The character fish are puppets mounted on 6'poles. For blocking purposes, the stage is a 3D cube divided into 18 blocking areas to accommodate scenes played high or low in the tank. There is a backdrop of aquatic vegetation, a filter pipe, a ground cloth painted to replicate the bottom gravel, a decorative castle and optional other aquarium decorations.

This play was first produced by the Viking Theater Company, Wareham, Massachusetts on February 26, 2009 with the following actors in the lead roles: Anthony Simmons as Robert Whitecheek-Tang; Moriah Bassett as Rayette; Maroby Walls as Elton; Eric Balboni as Stoney; Alex Couto as Twinky; Andrea Couto as Lorna; Kayla Rounds as Partita; Nick Weare as Pat Pufferfish and Vicky Van Hacht as Kimmy Echinaster.

<u>Scene 1</u>. [*The lights come up on the Sunday night closing number "One/Reprise" from "A Coral Line"*]

CAST. [*Singing, with movement.*]
> ONE SINGULAR CRUSTACEAN/
>
> EVERY LITTLE DIP SHE TAKES.
>
> ONE THRILLING COMBINATION/
>
> EVERY MOVE THAT SHE MAKES.
>
> ONE SMILE AND SUDDENLY
>
> NOBODY ELSE WILL DO;
>
> YOU KNOW YOU'LL NEVER BE LONELY
>
> WITH YOU KNOW WHO.
>
> ONE MOMENT IN HER PRESENCE/
>
> AND YOU CAN FORGET THE REST.
> FOR THE KRILL IS SECOND BEST/
>
> TO NONE, SON.
>
> OOOOH! SIGH! GIVE HER YOUR ATTENTION/
>
> DO...I... REALLY HAVE TO MENTION?

SHE'S THE... SHE'S THE... SHE'S THE... ONE!

[*They take their bows, but there is no applause, just the omnipresent sound of the filter.*]

TANG 1.   Did they see us? Did anyone notice?

BASSLET 1.   I dunno. I thought I saw a couple of people stop and watch on their way out.

TANG 2.   I'm just so tired of floundering around here and nobody really noticing all our effort.

BASSLET 2.   Quit your carping. I saw several people pointing and smiling.

TANG 3.   They were just pointing out the restrooms.

BASSLET 3.   No, I think they were totally hooked on our show!

BASSLET 4.   I'm certain Kimmy's choreography krilled 'em!

TANG 4.   Well, for my part, I was angling to impress them.

BASSLETS.   Well, your're no fin-omenon! [they laugh]

ELTON.   [breaking this up] All right, let's go. Break it up. Let's get some rest. Tomorrow we start with Othello.

[*the TANGS and BASSLETS swim off in all directions.*]

BASSLETS. [*sotto voce*] Clown…

[*Following the curtain call, STONEY approaches ELTON*]

STONEY.   Hey, Elton. Great show tonight, don't you think? I think it was our strongest show. I mean last night was ok, but there were some low points and the energy wasn't there, but tonight – I thought tonight was awesome, didn't you?

ELTON.   Ya think?

STONEY.   Well, yeah, I thought I was good and the chorus pulled it together pretty good.

ELTON.   If you say so, Stoney.

STONEY. Don't you think we were awesome tonight?

ELTON. Stoney, I thought this was our worst performance.

STONEY. Yeah, I guess so.

ELTON. I thought Twinky was like in another fish tank. I mean what was he thinking? He was totally chewing the scenery, and when he wasn't, he was as impressive as …sponge.

STONEY. But Rayette was good wasn't she Elton? I mean I think she's never looked better. All those spiney things and that caudal peduncle tonight was …[*pause*] woo hoo hoo! [*he shivers with excitement over the thought of RAYETTE*].

ELTON. Rayette sucked tonight, Stoney. Ok? She sucked, we sucked, you suck, they all suck.

BASSLETS. Suck. [*together, but not in unison*]

STONEY. Well, I suppose she was up on a line or two maybe here or there. Maybe her blocking was a little screwed up, but hey, turn down the sound and just look at her, right Elton? [He gyrates in an unbecoming way and makes woofing noises.]

BASSLETS. Woof. [*ELTON just stares at him.*]

ELTON. Well you can forget about her, Stoney, because she's sleeping with Whitecheek-Tang.

STONEY. With Robert!? Are you serious?

ELTON. Yup. How do you think she got Desdemona?

STONEY. Auditions?

ELTON. Right. They're living together behind the big castle. I suppose if I auditioned the way she did, I'd be Cassio instead of Stage Manager again.

STONEY. Stage Manager again, huh?

ELTON. Yeah… Stage Manager.

STONEY. That sucks.

BASSLETS. Sucksss.

STONEY. Elton, why didn't you talk to her like you were going to and let her know I liked her? Hey, wait a minute! What's Pufferfish going to say about this? He's supposed to be her guardian or something right?

ELTON. Right. That's right, Stoney. What will Pat Pufferfish say about this? That's the question. Sometimes I think a teeny tiny little thought man ages to seep into your teeny tiny little fish brain that's right on target.

BASSLETS. Stoopid.

STONEY. Yeah – what's Pat gonna say about Rayette moving in with Robert? I bet he'll be wild!

BASSLETS. Wild.

ELTON. We'll find out at tomorrow's production meeting, won't we, Stoney?

STONEY. Elton. You are wicked.

BASSLETS. Wickeddd.

Scene 2. [*Monday at a production meeting. PAT, TWINKY, STONEY, ELTON, LORNA, AND KIMMY are gathered center for a production meeting, to go over the upcoming production of Othello. The BASSLETS hover nearby.*]

PUFFERFISH. Ok, let's get started. We have a lot to go over and a short time to get everything ready. Where's the director?

ELTON. Robert? Well, looks like he's late.

STONEY. I guess he's not the only one late… hmmm. Looks like Rayette is not here either.

ELTON. Hmmmm the Director and the female lead.

STONEY. Missing

ELTON.   At the same time.

STONEY.   I wonder where they are.

PUFFERFISH.   What are you guys insinuating?

BASSLETS   Not too bright.

PUFFERFISH.   Is there something going on between Rayette and that Whitecheek-Tang?

BASSLETS.   I bet they're having a whale of a time!

ELTON.   Well, you must be the last one to know this, Pat, but yes.

STONEY.   They're living together

ELTON.   Behind the big castle.

STONEY.   Together

BASSLETS.   Redundant.

PUFFERFISH.   Why that …. [*he is fuming*]. I'll tear his scales off one by one. I'll snap every spine in his dorsal fin. I'll whack him so hard he'll have to back up to the surface to eat!

[*ROBERT joins the group.*]

ROBERT.   Sorry I'm late. What are we talking about?

BASSLETS.   You've haddock now! [*they laugh.*]

PUFFERFISH.   We're discussing your casting methods, evidently.

ROBERT.   Meaning?

PUFFERFISH.   Meaning you're sleeping with a young fish for which I am responsible and this after all I have done for you! You are nothing but a filthy opportunist…

BASSLETS.   Tunaaa…

PUFFERFISH.   Who will trade off someone's long standing support simply to destroy innocence like it was some chattel of yours for the using!

ROBERT. I do confess the vices of my blood, so justly to your grave ears I'll present hHow I did thrive in this fair lady's love. I told oft of triumphs on the stage- of fishly shows that once were all the rage - performances for the folk here at Sculch Cove; and by these tales did win this fish's love. This to hear would Rayette seriously incline: But still, Pufferfish chores would draw her thence: which ever as she could with haste dispatch. She'd come again, and with a greedy ear devour up my discourse: which I observing, took once a pliant hour, and found good means to draw from her a prayer of earnest heart that I would all my theater tales relate, whereof by parcels she had something heard, she loved me for the plays that I had done, and I loved her that she did favor them. This only, is the witchcraft I have used: Here comes the lady; let her witness it. [*RAYETTE arrives late and confirms his story. . .*]

RAYETTE. That I did love the fish to live with him, my downright violence and storm of fortunes may trumpet to the world: my heart's subdued even to the very quality of my lord: I saw Robert's visage in his mind, and to his honor and his valiant parts did I my soul and fortunes consecrate. So that, dear lords, if I be left uncast, and nightly he rehearse with maidens all, the depth with which I love him is bereft me, and I a heavy interim shall support by this sad consequence. Let me act for him! Let me learn from him! Let me live with him!

BASSLETS. Shakespeare...Whew! Oh my cod!

PUFFERFISH. Well, OK. Since you put it that way. I guess its fine with me. [*STONEY quickly draws ELTON aside.*]

STONEY. Did you hear that? Do you believe that? I mean all the guy does is quote some Shakespeare and he worms his way off the hook! I can't believe that! If I can't have Rayette Radiata, I'm going to drown myself.

ELTON. You're a fish.

STONEY.   I don't care. That is totally unfair! I mean it. I'm going to drown myself.

ELTON.   You can't drown yourself.

STONEY.   Watch me.

ELTON.   Relax. Robert Whitecheek-Tang is not the only one around here who can summon the power of the Bard.

STONEY.   What should I do? I'm ashamed to be so in love with her, but I really can't help myself.

ELTON.   Can't help yourself indeed; And so you need the help of one who has no such higher or lovelier aspiration than the pure revenge motive for which I was spawned! All power and authority lies in our wills. If we had not one scale of sensuality, the blood and baseness of our natures would lead us to the boldest and basest of achievements. Be a fish, Stoney. Drown yourself! Drown cats! Drown blind puppies! You are my friend and by every tough sinew that is within me, we will gut this out and we will prevail.

STONEY.   So I can count on you?

ELTON.   You can count on me.

Scene 3. [*Tuesday afternoon at rehearsal. TWINKY, RAYETTE, ELTON, LORNA, and STONEY are going over their lines.*]

ELTON.   OK, until Robert gets here, let's take it from Cassio's line – "the riches of the ship is come onshore."

TWINKY.   O, behold, the riches of the ship is come on shore! Ye men of Cyprus, let her have your knees. Hail to thee, lady! and the grace of heaven, Before, behind thee, and on every hand, Enwheel thee round!

RAYETTE.   I thank you, valiant Cassio. What tidings can you tell me of my lord?

TWINKY.   He is not yet arrived: nor know I aught But that he's well and will be shortly here.

RAYETTE.   O, but I fear—How lost you company?

TWINKY.   The great contention of the sea and skies parted our fellowship—But, hark! a sail, and guns!

BASSLETS.   They give their greeting to the citadel; this likewise is a friend.

TWINKY.   See for the news.

BASSLETS.   "Exit."

TWINKY.   [*To LORNA*] Welcome, mistress. Let it not gall your patience, good Iago, that I extend my manners; 'tis my breeding That gives me this bold show of courtesy. [*He Kisses LORNA.*]

STONEY.   Sir, would she give you so much of her lips as of her tongue she oft bestows on me, you'll have enough. [*The kiss continues...*]

BASSLETS.   Pig... That's enough... Let her breathe.

RAYETTE.   Alas, she has no speech.

ELTON.   Actually, she's saying a whole lot more than you might think. [*Aside*] The way he kisses and the way she likes it, I'll reel in as big a catch as Twinky. That's right. Smile at her. Charm her. These charms and smiles will soon enough cast you out of your role as Cassio. You'll be fin-ished and I'll be the dace in the hole!   [*ROBERT arrives.*]

ROBERT.   O my fair Radiata!

RAYETTE.   O my handsome White-cheeked Tang!

BASSLET 1.   Haddock about enough of this yet?

BASSLET 2.   Well, she sure has come out of her shell a little bit.

BASSLET 3.   Well, for a mussel bound fish like that, who wouldn't?

BASSLET 1.   Well, I wouldn't call him cod's gift to the aquarium.

BASSLET 2.   I'm sure he's an acquired taste.

BASSLET 3.   C'mon, it's not like he's looking for a brain sturgeon either.

BASSLETS   If you catch my drift. [*They laugh.*]

ROBERT.   Alright, let's settle down. We have a lot of work to do. Opening night will be here before you know it!

[*KIMMY ECHINASTER speaks up.*]

KIMMY.   Hey everybody, I'm having a cast party tonight and you're all invited. It's gonna be at 8 and we'll have it over….there! OK! So come and bring a friend and we'll have a halibut good time!

[*Everybody says "Yay", Yahoo!" and swims off in all directions, effectively ending the rehearsal.*]

ROBERT.   Oh boy, we gotta do something about the attention span around here. [*He swims off, leaving STONEY and ELTON.*]

ELTON.   Hey, news flash.

STONEY.   Yeah?

ELTON.   News flash. We've got a little problem.

STONEY   A problem? Honestly, Elton, you promised me…

ELTON.   Don't start crying, Stoney, wait'll you hear me out. I just got this on good word from a Tang who got it from another Tang who heard it from the Royal Gramma Basslets that Rayette is just playing Whitecheek-Tang for the leading role, but that she's really got it for … [*looks around,*]

STONEY.   Got it for whom?

ELTON.   Twin-ky!

11

STONEY. Twinky?!! Are you serious? Is she serious? How can anybody be serious about a Moorish Idol fish? He's gotta be THE MOST RIDICULOUS LOOKING FISH I KNOW!!

ELTON. Shhh! Calm down. The solution is simple, don't you see?

STONEY. Solution?

ELTON. Yes. There are too many fish standing between you and your beloved Rayette. You're going to have to *filter* them out.

STONEY. Filter them out?

ELTON. *Filter* them out. You know what I mean?

STONEY. I don't know I'm floundering a little here.

ELTON. Lookit. I'm not skating around the issue. You need to *filter* [*he nods toward the filter pipe*] out the competition.

STONEY. That's crappie.

ELTON. Well, are you a fish or are you a brine shrimp?

STONEY. I'll have to mullet over.

Scene 4. [*Tuesday night at the cast party. Music is playing. Some fish are "dancing"*]

BASSLET 1. Hey Kimmy, this is a pretty cool party.

KIMMY. Yeah. Thanks.

BASSLET 2. It's like everybody is here.

KIMMY. Well, everybody is here. It's an aquarium. There's no way to not be here, really.

TANG 1. Well, I came.

KIMMY. Yes you did.

TANG 2   I didn't want to miss it.

KIMMY.   Not much chance of that, was there?

BASSLET 1.   This is salmon chanted evening.

KIMMY.   Fer sure. Hey everybody, don't be koi, we've got plenty of stuff to eat!

TANG 1.   Whatcha got, Kimmy?

KIMMY.   Spirulina

BASSLETS.   Yum

KIMMY.   Algae

BASSLETS.   Yumm

KIMMY.   Plankton

BASSLETS.   YUMMM

KIMMY.   Knock yourself out. It's the same stuff we always have. Just go easy on the Beta-carotene. We know most of you drink like fish, but we don't want any DUI's – drinking until invertebrate!

BASSLETS.   Hee hee hee

TWINKY.   Wass zat sposta mean? [*obviously drunk*]

STONEY.   Whoa! Someone got an early start!

TWINKY.   Well whynnott?! Snot like there smush elsta do aroun' here.

STONEY.   Well, Kimmy said to lay off the beta carotene. Especially if you have an obvious problem

TWINKY.   Whoose zzz I hev a prollem?

STONEY.   Well, it's clear, you're not fish enough to hold your beta-carotene.

TWINKY.   Not fishynuff?

STONEY.   Not fish enough.

TWINKY. Not fishynuff?

STONEY. Not enough of a fish, yes, that is what I....

[*Blam! TWINKY slams into STONEY. The two fight.*]

BASSLETS. Fight! Fight! Fight! Fight! [*The fighting continues until ROBERT arrives and intercedes.*]

ROBERT. Hold it right there! I've just about haddock with this fighting!

ELTON. [*Who has been watching the fight*] Hold on there! Whoa! Twinky, Stoney! Did you forget that you are cast mates? Stop this fighting!

ROBERT. How did this get started? Is that how it is? We have a cast party so we can start pounding on each other? Elton – you were here? Who started this?

BASSLETS. Who? Who? Who did this?

ELTON. I don't know. I thought we were all friends here.

ROBERT. How about you, Twinky, do you know how this started? [*TWINKY is silent, just wobbling in place.*] Stoney, you are usually an easy-going fish. What brings this on?

STONEY. I think Elton had better tell you.

ROBERT. Look! I want to know right now who started this! This is ridiculous! Elton. Tell me who started this fight!

BASSLETS. Who? Who? Who did this?

ELTON. Well, I hate to take sides in these things.... But Twinky started it. Pretty much. Yeah.

ROBERT. I know, Elton, I can always trust you. Twinky – you are a pretty good actor, but a lousy drunk. I can't have these kinds of problems getting in the way of our opening. You are fired. You're out of the show.

BASSLETS. Oooohhhh! Voted off the island!!

ROBERT. Now get out of here, and stay out of my sight!

BASSLETS. Yer out!!

[*TWINKY swims off. ELTON follows him. The others return to partying.*]

ELTON. Pssst. Twinky. You listening?

TWINKY. Leave me alone.

ELTON. No seriously. Just take it easy.

TWINKY. Take it easy?! I blew it!

ELTON. Yeah, you kinda screwed up, but I have an idea that'll have you playing the lead again in no time.

TWINKY. Oh yeah? I doubt it.

ELTON. No seriously. I know Rayette really likes you. All you have to do is talk to her, and she'll get Whitecheek-Tang to reinstate you.

TWINKY. Fat chance.

ELTON. No seriously. This is no fluke. All you have to do is get Lorna to get Rayette to talk to you.

TWINKY. Sure. Whatever. I'm fried. Just call the Gorton's people, I'm a fish stick!

ELTON. Stop feeling so crappie. You can trust me.

TWINKY. I can count on you?

ELTON. You can count on me.

TWINKY. Well where is Lorna?

ELTON. Right over there, chum.

TWINKY. Oh! I flounder!

[*TWINKY swims over to LORNA LONGNOSE.*]

TWINKY. Hey Lorna, hey, umm yeah. I have to ask you a favor..

LORNA. What is it?

TWINKY. Well, ummm, you're real close to umm Rayette...

LORNA. Yeah. what's going on?

TWINKY. Well umm, she's with Robert and...

LORNA. Yeah?

TWINKY. And you heard how Robert kicked me out of the show, huh?

LORNA. Yeah, I did.

TWINKY. Well, umm, I was wondering...maybe you could umm talk to Rayette and possibly she could talk to me and then talk to Robert and put in a good word for me and get me my part back.

LORNA. Well, I, I...could try. I'm not sure she'll take the chance. He's pretty hot still.

TWINKY. Well I need you to do your best. Just try to get me this part back, cuz this...this is all I do. You don't know the scale of this...this is the only job I have. I can't go back to my old job of cleaning the ...screen on the tank...that was just dreadful and it tasted awful.

LORNA. I'm so sorry. I'll try my best. I'll put in a good word to Rayette, and hopefully she'll listen to me and hopefully she'll talk to you and hopefully she'll speak to Robert and hopefully he won't be so steamed by then and hopefully—

TWINKY. Just... do what you can.

LORNA. Sure.

TWINKY. Thanks.

[*RAYETTE appears at TWINKY'S side.*]

RAYETTE. I overheard you two talking.

TWINKY. Oh Rayette! Hi. So I guess you know about my problem, huh?

RAYETTE.   Yes, Twinky, but don't worry. Robert just hates that kind of stuff in the cast. He'll cool down.

TWINKY.   He seemed pretty sure he didn't want me in the cast anymore. I could sure use your help.

RAYETTE.   Be assured, Twinky, I'll do whatever I can for you. Don't worry. You guys will be laughing and joking together just like before.

TWINKY.   Oh, Rayette, I'll love you forever if you can do this for me!

RAYETTE.   Look, I know you really care for Robert. Any friend of his is a friend of mine!

TWINKY.   I just hope he doesn't hate me now.

RAYETTE.   Don't worry. When I whisper in his ear, magical things happen!

TWINKY.   Magical things, huh?

LORNA.   Rayette, here he comes!

TWINKY.   I'd better go.

RAYETTE.   Why? Stick around and hear what I have to say to him.

TWINKY.   Nah, he still looks pretty crabby. That look in his eye is freaking me out!

RAYETTE.   Well, you gotta do what you gotta do.

[TWINKY swims off.]

ELTON.   [*to ROBERT*] Hey, I don't like the looks of that!

ROBERT.   The looks of what?

ELTON.   Nothing, Nothing at all.

ROBERT. Wasn't that Twinky talking to Rayette just now?

ELTON.   Twinky? Nah. He wouldn't dare…ya think? Although he did kinda take off fast when he saw you coming…

17

ROBERT. I think it was Twinky.

RAYETTE. Hey Babe, I've been talking with someone that thinks you're pretty upset with him.

ROBERT. Who?

RAYETTE. Twinky! Our leading fish! Oh c'mon Sweetie, he made a mistake. Let him back in the show.

ROBERT. Was that him just now?

RAYETTE. Yes. He's so upset that you are mad at him. He feels really bad.

ROBERT. Oh, I don't even want to talk about it.

RAYETTE. Well when?

ROBERT. Why? [*She whispers in his ear.*]

ROBERT. Fine. He can have his part back. Anything for you snuggle-fins.

RAYETTE. But why don't you listen to his apology first, and make up your own mind.

ROBERT. Nah. If it's what you want, it's ok with me.

RAYETTE. Thanks, Sugar-lips! You're the best!

ROBERT. Listen, Rayette, why don't you go get all cozy in the castle, and I'll be home in a jiff, ok?

RAYETTE. You don't have to tell me twice! [*swims off.*]

ELTON. Robert…

ROBERT. What, Elton?

ELTON. When did Twinky know that you and Rayette were… a thing?

ROBERT. Right from the first. Before we even moved in, why?

ELTON. Just wondering…

ROBERT. What makes you ask?

ELTON. I didn't know if he knew her well, is all.

ROBERT.   O yeah, he actually knew her before me. He introduced us as a matter of fact.

ELTON. Did he indeed?!

ROBERT. Well, yeah. What's that supposed to mean? Can't he be trusted?

ELTON. Trusted?

ROBERT. Trusted. Don't you think Twinky can be trusted?

ELTON   What do I know?

ROBERT   Well, what do you think?

ELTON   What do I think?

ROBERT   What do you think? Why do you sound like a Parrot-fish? When you saw Twinky leaving Rayette, why did you say "I don't like that"?

ELTON. Did I say that?

ROBERT.   Yes, it's on page 15 of the script. What are you trying to say?

ELTON. Hey, you know we're buddies.

ROBERT. Yeah I know that.

ELTON. You know you can count on me.

ROBERT. Yeah, I know I can count on you. Now where are you going with all this?

ELTON. I think Twinky can be trusted.

ROBERT. Me too.

ELTON. But who can be trusted completely?

ROBERT.   Are you saying you don't think Twinky can be trusted completely around Rayette?

ELTON. If a fish could whistle – this would be the place.

ROBERT. By cod, I want to know what you are getting at.

ELTON. You'll never worm it out of me.

ROBERT. Ha!

ELTON. Hey, watch out for jealousy, is all. It's the green-eyed monster that can destroy the best couples.

ROBERT. What do I care about jealousy?

ELTON. Just watch Rayette around Twinky. You know what they say about the appetites of Lionfish!

ROBERT. You think so?

ELTON. Well, think of this… She didn't tell Pat Pufferfish until after she had moved in with you, am I right?

ROBERT. Yeah, that IS right..

ELTON. Keep an eye on her around Twinky. That's all I'm saying.

ROBERT. I have nothing to worry about. I trust Rayette.

ELTON. Well, I hope you never find out otherwise.

ROBERT. Find out?

ELTON. Nothing. I didn't mean it that way. Look. I better get going.

ROBERT. Yeah, Goodnight, Elton. Early rehearsal tomorrow.

ELTON. Yeah, look, don't give this little conversation a second thought.

ROBERT. Right… [*as ELTON swims off*] I really CAN count on him… [*RAYETTE rejoins ROBERT.*]

RAYETTE. Hey, Babe! I thought you were coming back to the castle! I've been waiting for you…

ROBERT. It's all my fault.

RAYETTE. Huh? What are you saying? What's the matter, Hun, not feeling well?

ROBERT.   I have a massive headache.

RAYETTE.   Ohh. I'm sorry. Here…let me soothe it with this special Egyptian Tiger Lotus that you gave me. [*She rubs him with the leaf.*]

ROBERT.   Your leaf won't work. [*He shakes the leaf off and it floats to the bottom.*] Come on, I'll go in with you.

RAYETTE.   I am sorry you're not feeling well, Babe.

[*ELTON, watching, grabs the leaf before the end of the scene.*]

Scene 5. [*Wednesday afternoon rehearsal.*]

ELTON.   Good morning Mr. Director.

BASSLETS.   Mr. Director!

ROBERT.   Elton.

BASSLETS.   Elton!

ELTON.   Sleep well?

ROBERT.   Hardly slept at all.

BASSLETS. [*singing*]

"COULDN'T SLEEP AT ALL LAST NIGHT.
DOOT DOOT DOO DOO DOOT!"

ELTON.   Awww. I'm sorry to hear that! Bad dreams?

ROBERT.   You could say that. Listen, Elton. Don't bother me with this stupid talk of Rayette and Twinky. I'm not going to hear anything of the kind, so just keep your thoughts to yourself and your mouth shut, got it? I don't want to hear another word on the subject unless you've got proof, you got that?

ELTON. Umm. Sure.

BASSLETS.   Sure.

ROBERT.   Good. Let's get on with rehearsal....

ELTON.   ...proof?

ROBERT.   Proof! Yesss! Proof! Don't' bother me unless you can prove something!

ELTON.   Ahem....

BASSLETS.   A-hemm!

ROBERT.   Why, what have you got?

ELTON.   Well, does talking in your sleep count?

ROBERT.   Who is talking in their sleep?

ELTON.   Why Twinky! He was saying it just last night way back in the plants, as if no one could hear him as he slept – 'Oh Rayette, Rayette, oh yes, oh Baby oh yes, Rayette, Rayette, oh my cod, I've haddock!'.... and so on.

BASSLETS.   Oh Baby! Oh my cod! [*and so forth.*]

ROBERT.   I'll kill them both.

ELTON.   Well, I'm not sure that that counts as proof, Robert. Maybe it's better to see if there's anything else... Don't you think so?

ROBERT.   Yeah, let's just see something else, Elton!

ELTON.   Like what? A kiss in private?

BASSLETS.   LIP LOCK!!

ROBERT.   Like sneaking a kiss...

ELTON.   How about locking lips for over an hour, not meaning anything by it?

ROBERT.   A sixty-minute lip lock, Elton, and not mean anything by it?! It is absolutely fishy that they would even do it and claim it had no meaning! How could they not be tempted to more?

BASSLETS.   Gouramis!

ELTON.   Forget it, they probably don't mean anything serious by it. It's nothing more than poor judgment. But if I gave my wife an Egyptian Tiger Lotus,—

ROBERT.   What about an Egyptian Tiger Lotus?

BASSLETS.   The leaf!

ELTON.   Why, then, it would be her Egyptian Tiger Lotus, and being hers, I would think she could give it to any fish she wanted.

ROBERT.   Yeah? Well, she owns her oviduct too. Can she give that to any fish she wants?

BASSLETS.   Ooooooh! Nasty.

ELTON.   Well… over 95% of all fishes are oviparous, meaning that fertilization takes place outside the body…

BASSLETS.   Spawn!

ELTON.   …but, as far as that Egyptian Tiger Lotus goes—

ROBERT.   If she's given him that Egyptian Tiger Lotus…

ELTON.   Well, so what?

ROBERT.   That won't go so good for them.

BASSLETS.   NOT- so good!

ELTON.   What, If I said I saw Twinky do you wrong? Or heard him say it?

ROBERT.   Did he say anything?

ELTON.   He did; but be assured, he would never admit to it.

ROBERT.   What did he say?

ELTON.   Well, that he … I don't know…

ROBERT.   What? what?

ELTON.   Lock—   [*The BASSLETS make kissy noises.*]

ROBERT.   With her?

ELTON. With her, on her; whatever.

BASSLETS. [*singing*]

"VOULEZ-VOUS NAGER AVEC MOI CE SOIR?"

ROBERT. [*to BASSLETS*]Shut up! [*To ELTON*] Lock with her! Lock with her! That does it! —lotus plant— confessions—lotus plant!—He'll confess, and then I'll crush him—Oh my cod!—that piece of carp!—

ELTON. Well look here, just you let me run this rehearsal while you hide over there behind the castle. I'll get him to confess with his own lips. He won't skate around the issue if he doesn't know you're listening!

ROBERT. Yes. That'll draw him out of his shell. Good plan, Elton. Where would I be without you?

BASSLETS. Yeahhhh, about that....

[*ROBERT moves off as STONEY and TWINKY enter.*]

TWINKY. [*singing*] "WHEN THE MOON HITS YOUR EYE LIKE A BIG PIZZA PIE, THAT A MORAY!"

STONEY. Hey, Twink, why pretend you can sing?

ELTON. OK, Boys, clam up. Let's pick it up where we left off yesterday...

STONEY. Ply Desdemona well, and you are sure on't. Speaking lower. Now, if this suit ...

ELTON. STOP!

BASSLETS. STOP!

ELTON. You don't *say* "Speaking lower", Stoney, you *just* speak lower. It's not a line, it's a stage direction!

BASSLETS. STUPID.

STONEY. OH. Sorry.

ELTON. And stop saying 'Sorry' every time you screw up.

STONEY. Sorry.

ELTON. It takes time out of rehearsal.

STONEY. OK, Sorry.

ELTON. Just go and don't say the stuff in italics.

STONEY. I don't have that line.

ELTON. No! It's not a line, I mean the things in italics are the stage directions. Don't say them.

STONEY. OK. Sorry.

ELTON. ...and stop saying sorry...

STONEY. [*pause*] Sorry.

ELTON. Take it from your line again.

BASSLETS. Which line?

ELTON. 'Ply Desdemona well...'

STONEY. Sorry. OK...Ply Desdemona well, and you are sure on't. [*Speaking lower.*] Now, if this suit lay in Bianca's power, How quickly should you speed!

TWINKY. Alas, poor caitiff! [*laughing.*]

ROBERT. [*Aside*] Oh I hate his laugh!

STONEY. I never knew woman love man so.

TWINKY. Alas, poor rogue! I think, i' faith, she loves me.

ROBERT. [*Aside*] Oh my cod! Double entendre! Is this the play 'Othello' or the real dynamic between Twinky and Rayette? Or is he Cassio speaking of Bianca? Or Twinky talking of Partita that way?

STONEY. [*to ROBERT*] Do you hear, Cassio?

ROBERT. [*Aside*] Now he's getting him to tell the story. I wonder if anyone put him up to this – Iago or .... Elton...but no. That would be un-canny.

25

STONEY. She gives it out that you shall marry hey: Do you intend it?

TWINKY. Ha, ha, ha!

ROBERT. [*Aside*] Do you liplock, Twinky? Do you?

TWINKY. I marry her! what? a customer! Prithee, bear some charity to my wit: do not think it so unwholesome. Ha, ha, ha!

ROBERT. [*Aside*] He laughs so easily because he has what he wants...

STONEY. 'Faith, the cry goes that you shall marry her.

TWINKY. Prithee, say true.

STONEY. I am a very villain else.

ROBERT. [*Aside*] Have you gotten with my Rayette?

TWINKY. This is the monkey's own giving out: she is persuaded I will marry her, out of her own love and flattery, not out of my promise. She was here even now; she haunts me in every place. I was the other day talking on the sea-bank with certain Venetians; and thither comes the bauble, and, by this hand, she falls me thus about my neck— So hangs, and lolls, and weeps upon me; so hales, and pulls me: ha, ha, ha!

ROBERT. [*Aside*] He's talking about how she lured him to our little corner of the aquarium! You will die for this!

TWINKY. Well, I must leave her company.

STONEY. Before me! look, where she comes.

TWINKY. 'Tis such another whore! albeit a perfumed one. [*PARTITA enters.*] What do you mean by this haunting of me?

PARTITA. Let the devil and his dam haunt you! What did you mean by that same leaf you gave me even now? [*She flips the Egyptian Tiger Lotus at him.*] I was a fine fool to take it. I must carry it around?—A likely leaf, that you should find it in your chamber, and not know who left it there! This is some minx's token, and I must carry it around? There; give it your hobby-horse: wheresoever you had it, I'll not have it.

TWINKY.   How now, my sweet Bianca! how now! how now!

ROBERT.   [*Aside*] My cod, that's my Egyptian Tiger Lotus!

PARTITA.   [*rubs on TWINKY*] And you come to my place tonight, [*to STONEY.*] Not you! [*She Exits.*]

STONEY.   Go after her!

TWINKY.   I'd better, or she'll announce to everyone my personal business!

STONEY.   Are you going to her place?

TWINKY.   Ohhh yesss!

ELTON.   OK, folks, I think we've seen about enough. That's a wrap. [*TWINKY and STONEY swim off.*]

ROBERT.   [*Swimming forth to meet ELTON.*] Enough, I'll say! How shall I murder him, Elton??

ELTON.   Did you see how he laughed?

ROBERT.   O yess!

ELTON.   And did you see the Egyptian Tiger Lotus?

ROBERT.   That was mine!

ELTON.   It's the only one in the tank! How he dotes on Rayette! She gave it to him, and he's given it to that dirty Partita.

ROBERT.   I will kill him slowly. And Rayette… so fine a fish! a sweet fish!

ELTON.   You're gonna have to forget that now.

ROBERT.   Yeah, let her rot, and die, and float to the top tonight; My heart is turned to stone. But the tank has never seen a sweeter fish.

ELTON.   No. that's not the way to think now.

27

ROBERT. Stuff her in the filter pipe! But she is so delicate, so fancy, so full of joy and adventure…

ELTON. She's a slut.

ROBERT. She's a mega-slut.

ELTON. That's too nice.

ROBERT. That's for sure, but still, the pity of it Elton! O Elton, the pity of it, Elton! [*He weakens.*]

ELTON. If you don't mind her doing every Tang and Basslet in the tank, then let her. If it doesn't bother you at all, it sure as heck won't bother them!

ROBERT. I will chop her into pieces! Cheat on me!

ELTON. She sucks.

ROBERT. With Twinky – a second rate actor.

ELTON. That's worse.

ROBERT. I won't let her eat. I'll starve her to death.

ELTON. Nah, don't do it that way. You might change your mind along the way. You have to stuff her in the filter pipe.

ROBERT. Yeah. That's how it has to be done.

ELTON. And as for Twinky, I'll take care of him. He'll be dead by midnight.

ROBERT. Excellent! Good. [*RAYETTE joins them.*]

RAYETTE. Hey, Babe, I'm sorry I missed rehearsal. How'd it go? [*He is silent.*] Hun? … Robert?

ROBERT. Let me see your eyes. Look in my face.

RAYETTE. What's going on?

ROBERT. [*To ELTON.*] Don't you have a job to do? Beat it! [*ELTON leaves.*]

RAYETTE. What are you getting at? You sound angry, but I can't for the life of me figure out why?

ROBERT. What are you?

RAYETTE. What am I? I'm your girlfriend, is that what you mean?

ROBERT. Swear to me that you aren't a slut.

RAYETTE. A slut?! I'm no slut!

ROBERT. Cod knows, you lie through your gills.

RAYETTE. Explain to me, Robert. What makes me a slut?

ROBERT. Oh Rayette, Get away from me!

RAYETTE. But why are you so upset with me, Babe? Is it something I said? I told you I was sorry for missing the rehearsal…

ROBERT. You could do anything to me — except cheat on me. That is the worst thing to bear!

RAYETTE. I hope you know that I have been true to you.

ROBERT. Oh YA! I wish I had never met you.

RAYETTE. What the heck have I done?

ROBERT. What have you done? Are you serious? You cheeky whore!

RAYETTE. You have no right to call me that!

ROBERT. Oh? You're not a whore?

RAYETTE. No! As a matter of fact, you are the only fish I have ever been with!

ROBERT. Oh, so you're not a cheap slut then…

RAYETTE. Not.

ROBERT. Well, excuuuse me! I've made a mistake here! I mistook you for my faithful girlfriend who just thought it was ok to get with every other fish in the tank!

RAYETTE. O, my cod! [*Swims off toward the filter pipe. He follows. ELTON and STONEY resume rehearsing.*]

ELTON. Robert asked me to go over the Othello lines with you in case we need an understudy. Do you think you can manage that?

BASSLETS. Liar.

STONEY. M-m-me? Understudy for Othello?

BASSLETS. Fat chance!

ELTON. Sure, I know it's a stretch, but Whitecheek-Tang is the boss, so I said I'd give it a whirl.

STONEY. I guess this is my big op-perch-tuna-ty, huh?
ELTON. Don't be koi. You want the job or not?

STONEY. Sure, sure. I'll give it a whirl.

ELTON. I'm waiting with baited breath.

BASSLETS. Hahahahaha

ELTON. Take it from his final speech with Desdemona…

STONEY. Ok. Ah balmy breath, that dost almost persuade justice to break her sword! One more, one more. Be thus when thou art dead, and I will kill thee, and love thee after. One more, and this the last: so sweet was ne'er so fatal. I must weep, but hey are cruel tears: this sorrow's heavenly; It strikes where it doth love. She wakes.

ROBERT. Right. [*He stuffs her in the filter pipe.*]

RAYETTE. [*Screaming.*] Aaaaaaaaahhhhhhhhh!!! [*She dies.*]

STONEY. What was that?

ELTON. Nothing, Stoney. Don't get in a stew about it.

STONEY. I heard something!

ELTON. Hey listen, Stoney, your reading just now was brilliant! I think you really should be moving up in this theater company.

STONEY. You think so?

ELTON. Oh yeah, you read that Othello with the skill of an amateur!

STONEY. Yeah? Ya think?

ELTON. Sure. I bought it.

STONEY. You did?

ELTON. Hook, line and sinker!

STONEY. Wow!

ELTON. You know the only problem though…

STONEY. There's a problem?

ELTON. Sure there's a problem … we talked about it before. Remember?

STONEY. Ahhh. Yeah… No.

ELTON. C'mon. It was back in Scene 3. I said you'd have to filter out the competition to get anywhere.

STONEY. Oh yeah. You did say that. I forgot. Sorry.

ELTON. Well, you were supposed to mullet over.

STONEY. And?

ELTON. And?

STONEY. What did you decide?

ELTON. No! You were the one who was supposed to think about it.

STONEY. Oh. Sorry.

ELTON. Alright, sucker. Listen up. If you're tired of angling to impress Pat Pufferfish with your talent, forget about it. The only way for you to get the lead role and hook up with Rayette is to stuff Twinky in the filter pipe. Got it?

STONEY. Gee. I … guess so.

ELTON. Good… Go… Do it… Now!

31

STONEY. Sorry! [*STONEY swims off.*]

Scene 6. [*Later Thursday night.*]

ROBERT.   Twinky slept with her. Ask Elton if it wasn't true. He knew it all.

LORNA.   Elton!

ROBERT.   Elton.

LORNA.   That she cheated on you?

ROBERT.   Yes, with Twinky.

LORNA.   Elton!

ROBERT.   Yeah, he was the one who told me first. He hates cheating and lying.

LORNA.   Elton!

ROBERT.   Why do you keep saying his name? I said Elton!

LORNA.   Elton said that she cheated on you.

ROBERT.   YES! I'm quite sure he knows what cheating is.

LORNA.   If he says she cheated on you, then he can rot in hell for all I care!

ROBERT.   Ha!

LORNA.   Go be your bad self, Robert. She deserved a lot better than the likes of you.

ROBERT.   You'd best shut up.

LORNA.   You have no power over me, fool! Help! Help! Robert has killed Rayette!! Help!!

[*Enter TANG 1, TANG 2, ELTON, and others*]

TANG 1.   What's going on here?

EMILIA   Oh, here you are, Elton. Good job! Getting others to do your murdering.

TANG 2.   What are you talking about?

LORNA.   Deny it if you call yourself a clownfish. He says you told him Rayette cheated on him. Did you tell him that?

ELTON.   I told him what I thought, that's all. He figured it out for himself.

LORNA.   Did you tell Robert that she cheated on him?

ELTON.   Yes.

LORNA.   YOU LYING SCUM! Did you say it was with Twinky?

ELTON.   Yes, with Twinky. You best shut your mouth now.

LORNA.   I will not shut my mouth. Rayette has been stuffed in the filter...

TANGS.   OH NO!!

LORNA.   [*to ELTON*] And you are the cause of it.

ROBERT.   Why, it's true!

ELTON.   You're crazy. Get out of here.

LORNA.   You can't get rid of me so easily, Elton.

ELTON.   You keep your mouth shut about things, Lorna.

LORNA.   The truth will come out, Elton.

ELTON.   Go on, get out of here now.

LORNA.   I will not. Elton took the Egyptian Tiger Lotus himself.

ELTON.   You whore!

LORNA. He gave it to Twinky

ELTON. You lie! [*He stuffs LORNA in the filter pipe.*]

LORNA.   AAAAAHHHHHHHH!!!!! [*Screaming. She dies.*]

ROBERT. You sneaky bastard! [*He stuffs ELTON in the filter pipe.*]

ELTON. AAAAAAAHHHHHHHH!!!!! [*Screaming. He dies.*]

[*Enter PUFFERFISH. TANG 3, TANG 4, TWINKY*]

PUFFERFISH. Where is this rash and most unfortunate fish?

ROBERT. I'm here. A shell of my former self.

PUFFERFISH   You, Robert Whitecheek-Tang. You were so good once. I don't know what to say. You are fired. You are no longer the director of this play or of this theater company. Twinky, you'll have to make sure that the show still goes up on time.

ROBERT. Wait! I want to say something before you go. I have done the theater some service, and everyone knows it. No more of that. I pray you, in your letters, When you shall these unlucky deeds relate, Speak of me as I am; nothing extenuate, Nor set down aught in malice: then must you speak Of one that loved not wisely but too well; Of one not easily jealous, but being wrought perplex'd in the extreme; of one whose hand, Like the base Indian, threw a pearl away Richer than all his tribe; of one whose subdued eyes, Albeit unused to the melting mood, Drop tears as fast as the Arabian trees Their medicinal gum. Set you down this; And say besides, that in a tank once, Where a malignant clownfish Beat a Whitecheek-Tang and traduced the play, I took by the throat the tragic fish, And ended him, thus. [*He stuffs himself into the filter pipe.*]

ROBERT. AAAAAAAHHHHHHHH!!!!! [*Screaming. He dies.*]

PUFFERFISH. O hell! Not another one.

KIMMY: Oh clownfish ghost who floats somewhere above, More fell than anguish, hunger, or the sea!

Look on the tragic loading of this pipe;
This is your work: the object poisons sight;
Let it be hid. O Twinky, keep the house,
And seize upon the fortunes of these fish,
For they succeed on you.
Direct this play, Rayette herself too pure and too naïve;
A gifted actress but no common sense
To move right in with her director fish
Is no replacement for audition scores.
Remains the foolish choice of Whitecheek-Tang;
Who knew not trust and yet he tried to love.
But must know now that love is just a bust
When nowhere can be found a shred of trust.

[*Fin.*]

The Cattish Play
The alley. The power struggle. The litter box.

Sick and tired of performing commercially successful yet banal musical material, a professional Equity company of cats experiences the upheaval of dissent, the treachery of ambition and the smothering kitty litter of death, as certain members of the company are hell-bent on producing much darker motifs.

Dramatis Felinae:

ALLIE, f, a tiger cat, actress
SAM, m, a grey cat, Director of "The Cattish Play"
GRAHAME, m, a grey cat, Producer of Catbox Productions
MITCH, m, a grey cat, a supporting actor
TC, m, a black cat, the male lead
BENNY, m, a very small blue cat, actor
CHOOCH, a very slow cat, actor
DIBBLE, m, a tiger cat, actor
BRAIN, m, an orange cat, the Stage Manager
FANCY FANCY, f, a cat with multiple personalities, actress
SPOOKY, m, a grey cat, actor
TRIXIE, f, a white cat, leading lady
PORTERHOUSE, m, a calico cat, extra

Setting: *The back of an alley. A wood fence runs along the back of the scene. The tops of city buildings are seen beyond. A dumpster is up right of center. Brick building corners with non-working doors bracket L and R. A telephone pole rises from up center. There are garbage cans near the fence left of center. Primary entrances are UL and UR behind the buildings, and UC from the dumpster, (which is accessible by an unseen opening in the fence). Litter is strewn about the playing area.*

Scene 1. [*Thunder and lightning is created by banging on the side of the trash can and screwing/unscrewing the light over the alley door, S.L. This is done a-vista by BRAIN, up on a ladder, and PORTERHOUSE, at the trash can SR. Enter UL FANCY FANCY, playing the roles of all three witches. The effect is rather comical as she jerks herself into three different postures throughout the dialogue. BRAIN and PORTERHOUSE watch from the side. BRAIN (the SM) and PORTERHOUSE (a company player) discuss the mental state of FANCY FANCY. BRAIN tells of the recent successes of TC in a rival production company. GRAHAME announces that TC will be named the new leading man of "Catbox Productions". PORTERHOUSE shares a knock-knock joke.*]

FANCY FANCY [*as 1st Witch*]. When shall we three meet again in thunder, lightning, or in rain?

[*as 2nd Witch*]. When the hurlyburly's done,

                When the battle's lost and won.

[*as 3rd Witch*]. That will be ere the set of sun.

[*as 1st Witch*]. Where the place?

[*as 2nd Witch*]. Upon the heath.

[*as 3rd Witch*]. There to meet with Macbeth.

[*as 1st Witch*]. Fair is foul, and foul is fair.

[*as 2nd Witch*]. Hover through the fog ...

[*as 3rd Witch*]. ... and filthy air.

[*She dances off, doing a funky Mata Hari style dance.*]

BRAIN. Hey Porterhouse, get a load of that!

PORTERHOUSE. I know what you mean, Brain. Fancy Fancy is the only cat I know that could play all three witches.

BRAIN. I mean, where does that *come* from?

PORTERHOUSE. Oh, she could seriously meet herself coming around the corner.

BRAIN. Multiple personalities?

PORTERHOUSE. And how!

BRAIN. Well, they say that paranoid schizophrenia is all it takes to make it big in theater.

PORTERHOUSE. Being dropped on your head as a kitten is all it takes to make it in theater.

BRAIN. How long has she been that way?

PORTERHOUSE. Ever since she ran away from home. Her owner used to crush up the lithium pills in her Meow Mix.

BRAIN. She ran away from home to do this?

PORTERHOUSE. Yeah, about six months ago.

BRAIN. Dang, six months of cold turkey, what's my name today, I'll take the box or the curtain, sanity free theater life!

PORTERHOUSE. Yeah, but she's hot.

BRAIN. Yeah.

PORTERHOUSE. Yeah.

BRAIN. Wait'll the new cat gets a load of her.

PORTERHOUSE. There's a new cat? I didn't hear that.

BRAIN. Sure, sure. Grahame is looking for a new leading man to spice up the dramatic tension around Catbox Productions. So he and Sam hired this cat named TC. He was with The Furball Theater before this.

PORTERHOUSE. What about Spooky? He's been the leading man for months and months. As long as any cat can remember!

BRAIN. Long in the tooth. Sam assured Grahame that Spooky could play good soldier with a new star in place.

PORTERHOUSE. So this TC is a star, huh?

BRAIN. The way I understand it the Furball Theater was going to go under. But TC really saved the day. He came out of nowhere and really started making things happen.

PORTERHOUSE. What kind of things?

BRAIN. Well for instance he was really killing with his reviews. The future of the theater was in doubt. They couldn't pay the mortgage, they couldn't fill the house, they couldn't keep up with the utilities. Despite all that, TC signed a contract, and vowed to turn things around there.

PORTERHOUSE. Wow, talk about disdaining your own fortune!!

BRAIN. Yeah, he totally carved out a name for himself and ripped it up.

PORTERHOUSE. The way I heard it, Spooky went over to the Furball Theater and auditioned for some role.

BRAIN. No! Yeah?

PORTERHOUSE. Yeah, and Grahame caught wind of it – so this must be his retribution – bringing TC over here to Catbox Productions. [*GRAHAME enters. The other two jump.*]

BRAIN. Grahame!

PORTERHOUSE. Grahame!

GRAHAME. Precisely. Steal away their leading cat for trying to steal ours, and demoting Spooky for his disloyalty. Shouldn't you two be busy doing something?

BRAIN. Yes sir…

PORTERHOUSE. Well, I'm working on the Porter's speech. Knock knock.

GRAHAME. Who's there?

PORTERHOUSE. Cash!

GRAHAME. Cash who?

PORTERHOUSE. Nope – this is a nut-free zone! [*Exeunt.*]

Scene 2. [*TC muses on the possibility of killing GRAHAME in order to be Producer. Thunder. FANCY FANCY enters.*]

FANCY FANCY [*as 1st Witch*]. Where hast thou been, sister?

[*as 2nd Witch*]. Killing mice.

[*as 1st Witch*]. Look what I have.

[*as 2nd Witch*]. Show me, show me.

[*as 3rd Witch*]. Here I have a bag of catnip, potent as any!

[*She tosses the catnip on the ground and starts playing with it, tossing it, rolling on it. It is when she is on her back, in the indignant throes of intoxication by the nepeta cataria that TC and SPOOKY enter.*]

TC.   I'm really excited about getting started with Catbox Productions.

SPOOKY.   Well, here we are. You can tell by the wither'd, wild and whacky Fancy Fancy in her witch get up.

TC.   So that's what you call that…

FANCY FANCY [*from the ground.*]

[*as 1st Witch*].   All hail, TC! hail to thee, Leading Cat!

[*as 2nd Witch*].   All hail, TC, hail to thee, award winning Director!

[*as 3rd Witch*].   All hail, TC, thou shalt be Producer hereafter!

[*TC glances over his shoulders for signs of GRAHAME or SAM.*]

SPOOKY.   What are you worried about, TC? Fancy Fancy might be a bit daft, but some say she has 'the gift'.

FANCY FANCY .   You're the new cat? TC? You're pretty hot looking upside down. [*She stands up.*] And a lot shorter than I had imagined, right side up.

TC.   [*aside*] So much for 'the gift'. [*to FANCY FANCY*] Well, I signed a contract, so I know I'm the leading cat, but say more about being director and even producer!

[*FANCY FANCY runs off.*]

SPOOKY.   Where'd she go?

TC.   Into the air!

SPOOKY.   Did she really say that stuff, or are we crazy?

TC.   You heard what I heard.

SPOOKY.   No, *you* heard what *I* heard.

TC.   No, *you*.

SPOOKY.   No, *you*!

TC.   Well even so, I have often thought about directing in one of these nine lives.

SPOOKY. It's weird how sometimes even the most whacked out weirdo will just walk up to you and start telling you your inner thoughts. I don't know if I would trust Fancy Fancy.

TC. [*Aside*] I don't know whether it's good or bad. I've had a lot of success on the stage, it only seems natural to want to move on to directing. Take more control over the creative process. Just imagine auditioning all those hopeful Tabbies [he laughs].

SPOOKY. Look, how our partner's rapt.

TC. [*Aside*] Better yet to be producer and art director, to begin to really pocket a few sardines for the future… so… maybe she is flighty, but she's got me thinking about the possibilities.

SPOOKY. C'mon TC, we need to get ready for rehearsal.

TC. Sorry, I was deep in thought.

SPOOKY. No prob. [*Exeunt.*]

Scene 3. [*BRAIN tells TRIXIE that the Producer, GRAHAME will be coming to the alley to watch her rehearsal with TC, the new leading man. A fish bone comes flying out of the dumpster, followed by TRIXIE.*]

TRIXIE. 'When he wanted to know more about what she said to him, that whack-job took off. Little do you know, boyfriend, that I heard every word! You are the new leading cat here. And you will be the director as well – maybe even producer, who knows? But do you think you can do any of this on your own? Do you think you have gotten anywhere in these nine lives without the subtle arrangements of your faithful girlfriend Trixie? You are too much of a kitten, TC. You are too willing to lap up the cream of human kindness and take the easy way. Wait'll I get my paws on you to scratch my ambition behind your ear and yowl you into some action with my tongue to

9

overcome your meekness – to become the wife of a producer! Muahahaha! [*She flops down and starts catwashing.* BRAIN *enters and stands next to* TRIXIE *for a moment, watching her.*]

TRIXIE. What are you staring at?

BRAIN. Grahame is coming to rehearsal tonight. He wants to see you and TC in action.

TRIXIE. You're kidding! Neither of us is even off book yet!

BRAIN. Tough kibbles. He's here, and he wants to see what he's paying for.

TRIXIE. Fine. Tell him he has a big surprise in store! [*Exit* BRAIN.] The raven himself is hoarse that croaks the fatal entrance of Grahame under my battlements. Come, you spirits that tend on mortal thoughts, unsex me here, and fill me from the crown to the toe top-full of direst cruelty! make thick my blood; Stop up the access and passage to remorse, that no compunctious visitings of nature shake my fell purpose, nor keep peace between the effect and it! Come and nurse from me, and take my milk for gall, you murdering ministers, wherever in your sightless substances you wait on nature's mischief! Come, thick night, and pall thee in the thickest smoke of hell, that my keen claw see not the wound it makes, nor heaven peep through the blanket of the dark, to cry 'Hold, hold!'

[*Enter TC. They move to embrace.*]

TRIXIE. Hi hon. I was just going over my lines.

TC. My dearest love, Grahame is coming to rehearsal to-night.

TRIXIE. And how long is he staying?

TC. Until tomorrow, I guess.

TRIXIE. He will never see tomorrow! Leave all the rest to me. [*Exeunt.*]

Scene 4. [*Rehearsal. The ensemble are seated around watching TC and TRIXIE in their debut with the company.*]

TC.   We will proceed no further in this business. he hath honor'd me of late; and I have bought golden opinions from all sorts of people, which would be worn now in their newest gloss, not cast aside so soon.

TRIXIE.   Was the hope drunk wherein you dress'd yourself? Art thou afeard to be the same in thine own act and valor as thou art in desire?

TC.   Prithee, peace. I dare do all that may become a man; who dares do more is none.

TRIXIE.   What beast was't, then, that made you break this enterprise to me? When you durst do it, then you were a tom; I have given suck, and know how tender 'tis to love the kit that milks me. I would, while it was smiling in my face, have pluck'd my nipple from his boneless gums, and dash'd the brains out, had I so sworn as you have done to this.

TC.   If we should fail?

TRIXIE.   We fail! But screw your courage to the sticking-place, and we'll not fail. When he is asleep, his two assistants will I with catnip and cream so convince that memory, when in swinish sleep their drenched natures lie as in a death, what cannot you and I perform upon the unguarded leader?

TC.   Away, and mock the time with fairest show. false face must hide what the false heart doth know.

[*First GRAHAME, then SAM and all the rest rise, applauding the performance of the pair, little guessing how earnest their motivation.*]

GRAHAME.   Bravo, Brava! I think our fortunes have taken a turn tonight! Welcome to Catbox Productions, my friends. Let's call it a night and start with Act 2 in the morning.

11

[*All begin to gather and leave.*]

PORTERHOUSE.   Knock knock.

BRAIN.   Who's there?

PORTERHOUSE.   Honey bee!

BRAIN.   Honey bee who?

PORTERHOUSE.   Honey bee a dear and change that cat box! [*Exeunt.*]

TC.   [*crossing slowly downstage*] Is this a claw which I see before me, greater than the one on my paw? [*He bats at it several times.*] I can't claw you, but I can still see you! Are you some phantom claw that can be seen but not batted? A claw of the mind – coming from my fevered cat-brain? [*A bell rings.*] I've got to get this done; the bell reminds me. Don't listen, Grahame, it is your invitation to either heaven or hell! [*Exit.*]

Scene 5.   [*Even later. Owls and crickets are heard. Enter TRIXIE.*]

TRIXIE.   Quiet! Quiet, damn crickets! What if they wake up and it isn't done? If Grahame didn't look like my own father all curled up with his tail over his eyes, I would have done it myself! [*Enter TC.*] TC!

TC.   It's done. Did you hear anything?

TRIXIE.   Just the owl scream, and the crickets cry.

TC.   Who is sleeping next to Grahame behind the dumpster?

TRIXIE.   It is Sam, I think. Did you kill him too?

TC.   This is a sorry sight. [*Looking at his paws.*]

TRIXIE.   Don't be stupid. You worry too much. Worry will drive you mad.

TC. But this blood!

TRIXIE. Look, here's some water. Let's wash this filthy gore from your paws. [*Knocking is heard. TC arches up.*]

TC. Who is knocking? Why does ever sound make me jump?

TRIXIE. My paws are red now too; but I shame to wear a heart so white. [*Knocking again.*] I hear a knocking by the fence. Let's get out of here. [*Exeunt.*]

Scene 6. [*Early Morning. Knocking is heard. Enter PORTERHOUSE.*]

PORTERHOUSE. Knock, knock, knock! Who's there, in the name of Grumpy Cat!?

[*Enter MITCH and DIBBLE.*]

MITCH. What time did you finally lie down so that you are still sleeping?

PORTERHOUSE. Calm down, man. We're actors. We go to bed at dawn and get up at noon. At the earliest.

MITCH. Have you seen TC this morning?

PORTERHOUSE. Is that a trick question? Do my eyes look like they've seen much this morning? [*Enter TC.*]

MITCH. Hey, TC.

DIBBLE. Hey, TC

TC. Hey, Mitch. Hey, Dibble.

PORTERHOUSE. I got up for this dialogue to happen?

MITCH. Is Grahame up yet?

TC. Not. I don't expect him to be up for [*to the audience*] quite... some... time...

13

MITCH.   That's strange. He told me to come early today because he wanted to start Act 2. I'll go see if he's awake.

[*Exits behind dumpster.*]

DIBBLE.   The night has been unruly. where we lay. Our kitty litter is strewn all around; and, as they say, meowings heard in the air; you could hear strange cat screams all night long.

TC.   It was a bad night all around. [*Re-enter MITCH.*]

MITCH.   O horror, horror, horror! I can't even begin to describe!

TC and DIBBLE.   What's the matter?

MITCH.   Murder!

TC.   What?!

DIBBLE.   Who, Grahame?

MITCH.   Go look behind the dumpster and see for yourself! [*Exeunt TC and DIBBLE.*] Wake up! Wake up! Murder! Murder!

TRIXIE.   [*Entering*] What the heck is going on? What's all the flap about? Can't a cat get a decent night's sleep? Who's responsible for this racket?

MITCH.   Oh Trixie, I can't even tell you. It's too horrible. [*Enter SPOOKY.*] Oh Spooky, Spooky, Grahame's been murdered!

TRIXIE.   What, in our alley?

SPOOKY.   Say it ain't so, Mitch!   [*The COMPANY enters.*]

SAM.   What is happening?

MITCH.   Your boss's murder.

SAM.   By whom?

DIBBLE.   That's a very good question Sam. His throat was cut.

SPOOKY. Let's put our heads together and figure out who did this bloody work. I won't stand for this kind of malice amongst enlightened cats.

MITCH. Me neither!

DIBBLE. Me neither!

BRAIN. Me neither!

TC and TRIXIE. Us neither!

FANCY FANCY, ALLIE, BENNY and CHOOCH. Us neither!

[*Exeunt all but PORTERHOUSE and SAM.*]

PORTERHOUSE. What about you? What's your story?

SAM. I'm outa here, man. They're just gonna accuse me because I was next in line to be producer. The last thing I need to stick around for is vigilante justice! I'm gonna head across the city until things cool down a little.

PORTERHOUSE. Did you kill Grahame?

SAM. Don't be stupid.

PORTERHOUSE. But what about the play?

SAM. Hey, I've got more important problems to worry about.

PORTERHOUSE. Well, good luck. Oh and hey... Knock knock.

SAM. Who's there?

PORTERHOUSE. Madame!

SAM. Madame who?

PORTERHOUSE. Madame acting career is going down the tubes!

SAM. Especially in a play like this! [*Exeunt.*]

15

Scene 7. [*The next day. TC and SPOOKY are talking.*]

TC. I'm having a little cast get together tonight, and I'd like you to be there.

SPOOKY. Whatever.

TC. You going somewhere this afternoon?

SPOOKY. Yup.

TC. Where you off to?

SPOOKY. As far as I can roam between now and supper...

TC. Don't miss the cast part... er... get together.

SPOOKY. Whatever.

TC. I hear Sam is across town with my former theater company. What could look more suspicious than that? Here we are, all in mourning for Grahame, and Sam high tails it across town.

SPOOKY. Whatever.

TC. Is Benny going with you?

SPOOKY. Yup.

TC. Well have a swell afternoon! [*SPOOKY exits.*] Chooch!! [*CHOOCH scurries in.*] Have you been thinking about what I told you? You know Spooky thinks you are the one that killed Grahame. He told me as much himself. Look right at me... Spooky – is – your – enemy.

CHOOCH. Dat's true.

TC. But you know what I think, Chooch?

CHOOCH. What? What do you think, Boss?

TC. I think Spooky is the one that did it!

CHOOCH. Ohhh yeahhh! He mus' be da one dat did it!

16

TC. Do you know what that makes Spooky, Chooch?

CHOOCH. What? ... no, I got it! ... no... I don't... what does dat make Spooky?

TC. Look right at me, Chooch. That makes Spooky – your – enemy – and – my -- enemy too. And I would love for him to be all gone.

CHOOCH. You want him to be all gone, Boss?

TC. That's right, Chooch. Now what are you going to do about that?

CHOOCH. What?

TC. What are you going to do about making Spooky all gone?

CHOOCH. What?

TC. You are going to make him all gone!

CHOOCH. Ohhhh! Chooch is going to make Spooky all gone! Huh huh huh.

TC. And Benny too.

CHOOCH. Benny is going to make Spooky all gone?

TC. No, Chooch, you are going to make both Spooky and Benny all gone.

CHOOCH. Ohh. Ok, Boss.... [*pause*]

TC. You can go now, Chooch.

[*CHOOCH crosses to playing area D.R.*]

CHOOCH. I smell cats. I wish I knew how to turn on dis light. It has to be them, on account of everybody else is at da fancy feast. Mmmmm, Fancy Feast!

[*SPOOKY and BENNY appear D.R.*]

BENNY. Gee, Spooky, it sure is dark! There's no moon tonight.

SPOOKY. That's because it's cloudy. It's gonna rain.

CHOOCH. LET IT COME DOWN!!! [*He jumps SPOOKY.*]

SPOOKY.   Oh! Run, Benny! Run! Chooch, you treacherous idiot! [*Dies. BENNY escapes.*]

CHOOCH.   Dat wasn't easy in da dark! [*Exits.*]

Scene 8. [*TC and TRIXIE welcome the guests to their fancy feast. CHOOCH appears at the side.*]

TC.   Yuk it up, cats, there's plenty of catnip to go around... [*Approaching CHOOCH.*] There's blood on your paws.

CHOOCH. There is? Oh! There is. I think it belongs to ah...to ahh... .

TC.   Is he gone?

CHOOCH. Is who gone?

TC.   Look me right in the face, Chooch. Did you take care of Spooky?

CHOOCH. Well, I didn't take care of him, but I killed him.

TC.   And Benny too?

CHOOCH. Did Benny kill Spooky too?

TC.   No, Chooch, did you kill Benny too?

CHOOCH. Ahhh. Ahhh. I gotta think about dat one, Boss.

TC.   Well don't take all night.

CHOOCH. For what?

TC.   To think it over.

CHOOCH. Think what over?

TC.   Chooch, look right at me. Did you kill Benny too.

CHOOCH.   No. Benny high-tailed it out of there.

TC.   All right, get out of here and wash yourself.

CHOOCH.   Do I smell bad?

TC.   Well, yes, but it's your bloody paws I'm worried about.

CHOOCH.   Ohhh yeah!... [*CHOOCH exits.*]

TRIXIE.   TC, why don't you offer a toast to our guests?

DIBBLE.   Yeah, TC, sit with us!

[*The GHOST OF SPOOKY enters, sits in TC's place. TC arches up.*]

TC.   The table's full.

DIBBLE.   Here's your spot right here, TC!

TC.   Where?

DIBBLE.   Right here! Good lord! What's got you spooked?

TC.   Who has done this?!

DIBBLE.   Done what, TC?

TC.   [*To the GHOST OF SPOOKY*] YOU CAN'T SAY I DID IT!!! DON'T SHAKE YOUR BLOODY PAWS AT ME!

DIBBLE.   Yo, cats, let's scram. TC is off his rocker.

TRIXIE.   No, no, chill, cats. This nonsense will pass. He'll get over whatever's freaking him out. Don't pay any attention or he'll go all skittish. Eat, eat. There's plenty to go around. [to TC] What the actual hell??

TC.   [*quietly, to TRIXIE*] Hell indeed, looking at this bloody apparition!

TRIXIE. Why are you making these stupid faces? You look like you're straining in the cat box!

TC.   Look upon this turd yourself! [*indicating the spot where GHOST OF SPOOKY has just vanished*] He was just here!

19

TRIXIE. Idiot.

TC. I must have had a bad mouse.

TRIXIE. Look. Act normal, would you? You're ignoring our party guests.

TC. Sorry. Sorry. [to the others] Show's over, folks. Nothing to see here. Who's having a good time? Here's to good friends and great theater! [*All mumble "good friends...great theater..." and put their heads down in water bowls. GHOST OF SPOOKY reappears at this moment. TC shouts*] Holy spit!!! [*All cats jerk upwards and spray water into the air.*] Disappear! Disappear!! DISAPPEAR!!! [*GHOST OF SPOOKY vanishes as all look around.*]

TRIXIE. [*Laughing hollowly*] Ahh TC, you old trickster. He loves to make everybody spray like that. Good one! Ha ha ha...

TC. What's wrong with you that you can look at such horrible apparitions and make jokes about it?

DIBBLE. What apparitions, TC?

TRIXIE. Don't encourage him. That's it. Everybody out.

DIBBLE. [*to TC*] I ahhh... hope you start feeling better... I guess. [*Exeunt all but TC and TRIXIE.*]

TC. Wow. What the heck was that.

TRIXIE. Yeah. I was wondering the same thing.

TC. I must be overtired.

TRIXIE. ...or something... [*Exeunt.*]

Scene 9. [*Rehearsal. Chanting, FANCY FANCY stirs a trash can/cauldron. She channels warnings to TC to beware MITCH, to "fear none of litter born," to fear nothing until catnip comes to the Alley. TC decides to murder Mitch's wife Allie and her kittens. Thunder. Enter the three Witches.*]

FANCY FANCY [*as first witch*]. Double, double, toil and trouble. Fillet of a fenny snake, In the cauldron boil and bake.

[*as second witch*]. Eye of newt and toe of frog, Wool of bat and tongue of dog.

[*as third witch*]. Adder's fork and blind-worm's sting, Lizard's leg and owlet's wing. Double, double toil and trouble; Fire burn, and cauldron bubble.

[*Enter BRAIN. to Fancy Fancy*]. O well done! I commend your pains; and every one shall share i' the gains.

FANCY FANCY.   What the hell are you doing?

BRAIN.   Oh. The actress we hired to play Hecate was hit by a car, so I'm just standing in.

FANCY FANCY [*stares at him blankly, then*] That's hella unlucky.

BRAIN.   Yeah...

FANCY FANCY.   Yeah...

BRAIN. [*pause*] And now about the cauldron sing, live elves and fairies in a ring, enchanting all that you put in.

FANCY FANCY.   By the pricking of my thumbs, something wicked this way comes.

[*Enter TC.*]

TC.   How now, you secret, black, and midnight hags! What is't you do?

FANCY FANCY.   A deed without a name.

TC.   I conjure you, by that which you profess, howe'er you come to know it, answer me.

FANCY FANCY [*as first witch*].. Speak. [*as second witch*].Demand.

[*as third witch*]. We'll answer. Say, if thou'dst rather hear it from our mouths, or from our masters?

TC. Call 'em; let me see.

FANCY FANCY.   Pour in sow's blood, that hath eaten her nine farrow; grease that's sweaten from the murderer's gibbet throw into the flame. Come, high or low; thyself and office deftly show! [*BRAIN, at right, makes thunder.*]

TC. Tell me, thou unknown power—

FANCY FANCY. He knows thy thought. Hear his speech, but say thou nought.

BRAIN. TC! TC! TC! beware Mitch; Beware the tom cat. Dismiss me. Enough.

TC. Mitch?! Really, Brain??

BRAIN. That's what it says here.

TC. Whate'er thou art, for thy good caution, thanks; Thou hast harp'd my fear aright. but one word more—

FANCY FANCY. He will not be commanded. here's another, more potent than the first. [*Thunder.*]

BRAIN. TC! TC! TC! Be bloody, bold, and resolute; laugh to scorn the power of cats, for none of litter born shall harm TC.

TC. Let me see that! [*BRAIN shows him his book.*] That's weird. Then live, Mitch! What need I fear of thee? [*Thunder.*] What is this that rises like the issue of a lion?

BRAIN. Be lion-mettled, proud; and take no care who chafes, who frets, or where conspirers are. TC shall never tread death's valley 'till catnip comes to this here alley!

TC. You have got to be kidding me, Brain! [*BRAIN hastily shows TC his book again. TC, reading...*] "There is none extant to make the catnip plant to unfix his earth-bound root? It seems the point is moot!" Yet tell me, shall Spooky's kitten issue ever reign in this kingdom?

FANCY FANCY.   Seek to know no more.

TC.   I will be satisfied. deny me this, and an eternal curse fall on you!

FANCY FANCY [*as first witch*]. Show! [*as second witch*]. Show!

[*as third witch*]. Show! Show his eyes, and grieve his heart; Come like shadows, so depart!

[*SPOOKY as a ghost, and BENNY enter and do a freakishly comical, dance all around TC throughout his soliloquy.*]

TC.   Thou art too like the spirit of Spooky. down! Thy whiskers do sear mine eye-balls. And thy fur, thou other gold-bound brow, is like the first. A third is like the former. Filthy hags! Why do you show me this? A fourth! Start, eyes! What, will the line stretch out to the crack of doom? Horrible sight! Now, I see, 'tis true; For the blood-bolter'd Spooky smiles upon me, and points at them for his. [*SPOOKY and BENNY dive into the dumpster UC. The spell is broken. To FANCY FANCY*] What, is this so?

FANCY FANCY.   Ay, sir, all this is so. but why stand you thus amazedly? [*Exits.*]

TC.   Where are they? Gone? Come in, without there! [*Enter DIBBLE.*] I did hear the galloping of paws. who was't came by?

DIBBLE.   'Tis two or three, my lord, that bring you word Mitch has fled the alley.

TC.   Fled the Alley!

DIBBLE.   Ay, my good lord, fled the Alley.

TC.   Time, thou anticipatest my dread exploits. the family of Mitch I will surprise; Seize upon them; give to the edge o' the sword his wife, his kits, and all unfortunate souls that trace him in his line. [*Exeunt.*]

23

Scene 10. [*DIBBLE brings ALLIE the news that MITCH has fled the Alley and to warn her to run for her life, but right after him comes CHOOCH, who kills BENNY and ALLIE. Enter ALLIE, BENNY, and DIBBLE.*]

ALLIE.   What had he done, to make him fly the alley?

DIBBLE.   You must have patience, madam.

ALLIE.   He had none. His flight was madness. when our actions do not, our fears do make us traitors.

DIBBLE.   You know not whether it was his wisdom or his fear.

ALLIE.   Wisdom! to leave his wife, to leave his kittens, his mansion and his titles in a place from whence himself does fly? He loves us not; He wants the natural touch. for the poor wren, the most diminutive of birds, will fight, Her young ones in her nest, against the owl.

DIBBLE.   Cruel are the times. I take my leave of you. [*Exits.*]

BENNY.   Was my father a traitor, mother?

ALLIE.   Ay, that he was.

BENNY.   What is a traitor?

ALLIE.   Why, one that swears and lies.

BENNY.   And be all traitors that do so?

ALLIE. Every one that does so is a traitor, and must be hanged.

BENNY.   Who must hang them?

ALLIE.   Why, the honest cats.

BENNY. Then the liars and swearers are fools, for there are liars and swearers enough to beat the honest cats and hang them.

ALLIE.   Now, God help thee, poor pussy! [*Enter CHOOCH.*] What is this face?

CHOOCH.   Where is your husband?

24

ALLIE.   I hope, in no place so unsanctified where such as thou mayst find him.

CHOOCH.   He's a traitor.

BENNY.   Thou liest, thou shag-hair'd villain!

CHOOCH.   What, you egg! [*Slicing him with his claw.*]

BENNY.   He has kill'd me, mother. run away, I pray you! [*Dies. Exit ALLIE, crying 'Murder!' Exit CHOOCH, following her.*]

Scene 11. [*Porterhouse offers a knock-knock joke. Porterhouse tells Brain of Trixie's sleep-walking... Trixie walks and talks in her sleep, revealing guilty secrets.*]

PORTERHOUSE.   Knock knock

BRAIN.   Who's there?

PORTERHOUSE.   I... play... with... mop!

BRAIN.   I play with mop who?...

[*PORTERHOUSE dissolves into giggles. They are interrupted by TRIXIE, sleepwalking.*]

TRIXIE.   Out, damned spot! out, I say!—One. two. why, then, 'tis time to do't.—Hell is murky!—Fie, my lord, fie! a tomcat, and afeard? What need we fear who knows it, when none can call our power to account?—Yet who would have thought the old cat to have had so much blood in him. Mitch had a wife. where is she now?— What, will these paws ne'er be clean?—No more o' that, my lord, no more o' that. you mar all with this starting. Here's the smell of the blood still. all the perfumes of Arabia will not sweeten this little paw. Oh, oh, oh! Wash your paws, put on your nightgown; look not so pale.—I tell you yet again, Spooky's

25

buried; he cannot come out of his grave. To bed, to bed! there's knocking at the gate. come, come, come, come, give me your paw. What's done cannot be undone.—To bed, to bed, to bed! [*She climbs into the dumpster.*]

Scene 12. [*TC hears that his cast-mates are abandoning him, that others are approaching, and that TRIXIE is soul-sick, but he tries to convince himself that he has nothing to fear, and prepares to fight. Enter TC, DIBBLE, and others.*]

TC.   Our dumpster's strength will laugh a siege to scorn. here let them lie 'till famine and the ague eat them up. [*A meow comes from the dumpster.*] What is that noise?

DIBBLE.   It is the cry of women, my good lord. [*He goes to peer into the dumpster.*]

TC.   The time has been, my senses would have cool'd to hear a night-shriek; and my fell of hair would at a dismal treatise rouse and stir as life were in't. I have supp'd full with horrors; Direness, familiar to my slaughterous thoughts cannot once start me. [*to DIBBLE*] Wherefore was that cry?

DIBBLE.   Trixie, my lord, is dead.

TC.   She should have died hereafter; There would have been a time for such a word. To-morrow, and to-morrow, and to-morrow, creeps in this petty pace from day to day to the last syllable of recorded time, and all our yesterdays have lighted fools the way to dusty death. Out, out, brief candle! Life's but a walking shadow, a poor player that struts and frets his hour upon the stage and then is heard no more. it is a tale told by an idiot, full of sound and fury, signifying nothing.

[*Enter PORTERHOUSE.*] Thou comest to use thy tongue; thy story quickly.

PORTERHOUSE.   As I did stand my watch upon the fence, I look'd down the street, and before long, I saw the catnip bush was moving hence.

TC.   Liar and slave!

PORTERHOUSE.   Within three blocks may you see it coming; I say, a moving hedge!

TC.   I begin to doubt the equivocation of the fiend that lies like truth. 'Fear not, till catnip bush do come to this alley.' and now a bush comes down the street. Arm, arm, and out! Ring the alarum-bell! Blow, wind! come, wrack! at least we'll die with harness on our back. [*Exeunt.*]

Scene 13. [*Mitch and TC do battle. TC, tipsy from inhaling catnip, boasts that he cannot be harmed by "one of litter born," but MITCH replies that he was "from a pet shop, untimely sold." They fight on and Mitch kills TC. SAM and the surviving cats enter. He is hailed as the new Producer of Catbox Productions, whereupon he rewards MITCH as the new Leading Man. PORTERHOUSE asks if this would be a good time for a knock-knock joke. Enter TC.*]

TC.   They have tied me to a fight; Too much catnip is my plight; I cannot walk in a straight line, but, cat-like, you will see that I am fine! [*Enter MITCH.*]

MITCH.   Turn, hell-hound, turn! [*They fight.*]

TC.   Thou losest labor. as easy mayst thou the empty air with thy keen claw impress as make me bleed. I bear a charmed life, which must not yield, to one of litter born.

27

MITCH.   Despair thy charm; and let the angel whom thou still hast served tell thee, Mitch was from a pet shop untimely sold.

TC.   [*Jumps back.*] Accursed be that tongue that tells me so, I'll not fight with thee.

MITCH.   Then yield thee, coward!

TC.   I will not yield, to kiss the ground before young Sam's feet, and to be baited with the rabble's curse. Though catnip bush be come to this alley, and thou opposed, being of no litter born, yet I will try the last. Lay on, Mitch, and damn'd be him that first cries, 'Hold, enough!' [*Exeunt, fighting. There is a pause. Enter SAM, BENNY, CHOOCH, DIBBLE, BRAIN, FANCY FANCY and PORTERHOUSE.*]

SAM.   I would the friends we miss were safe arrived.

BRAIN.   Some must go off. and yet, by these I see, so great a day as this is cheaply bought.

SAM.   Mitch is missing, and your noble friend.

DIBBLE.   Spooky, my lord, has paid an actor's debt.

SAM.   Then he is dead?

BRAIN.   Ay, and brought off the stage.

DIBBLE.   Why then, God's actor be he! Had I as many kittens as I have hairs, I would not wish them to a fairer dispatch.

MITCH. [*Re-entering with TC's head.*]   Hail, Producer! for so thou art. Behold, where stands the usurper's cursed head. the time is free. Hail, Head of Catbox Productions!

ALL.   Hail, Head of Catbox Productions!!

SAM.   My fellow thespians, henceforth be stars, the first that ever this theater in such an honor named. What's more to do, which would be planted newly with the time, as casting more of our friends to mount the show "All's Well That Ends Well". Let us put in our distant memory the cruel castmates of this dead butcher and his fiend-like lady, who, as 'tis thought, by self and violent claws took off her life in yon dumpster; this, and what needful else that calls upon us, by the grace of Grace, we will perform in measure, time and place. so, thanks to all at once and to each one, whom we invite to see us mount this show.

PORTERHOUSE.   Knock knock?

SAM. Who's there?

PORTERHOUSE.   Mayonnaise!

SAM. Mayonnaise who?

PORTERHOUSE.   Mayonnaise a lot a dead cats up in here!

[*Fade*   *to*   *black*.]

Fowl Play

The power, the passion, the poultry.

The Chicken Coop is home to two feuding groups, the Football Team and the Drama Club. In response to the constant fighting between members of these groups, the Principal of the Chicken Coop has issued an edict that will impose expulsion on anyone caught fighting. Against this backdrop, young Danny on the football team falls for Sandy, the drama club's leading lady (about to play Juliet in the upcoming play.) Together, they live out the famous final scenes of Shakespeare's star-crossed lovers.

The following music is referenced in the script. Rights for these pieces must be arranged separately. "*Psycho Chicken*", by Douglas Forman/Michael Girard/David Byrne, Bleu Disque Music Co. Inc.; and "Chicken Dance Polka", by Werner Thomas, Stanley Mills, publisher, New York, NY.

Dramatis Gallinulae.

PULLET, The Principal
DANNY, Quarterback of the Coop's football team
BUCKEYE, Danny's friend and teammate
CAMPINE, HOUDAN, WYANDOTTE, football players
LEGHORN, an intellectually challenged football player
ANCONA, ARAUCANA, BANDARA, Cheerleaders
SANDY, a drama chick
SILKIE, her friend
BUTTERCUP, CATALANA, LAMONA, female drama chickens
DORKING, a bantam actor cast as Romeo
FRIZZLE, the understudy for Romeo
ORPINGTON, another acting rooster

This play was first produced by the Viking Theater Company, Wareham, Massachusetts on February 26, 2004. The roles were originated by, Sara McGregor as Principal Pullet; Jabe Ziino as Danny; Kevin Johnson as Buckeye; Jon Nickerson as Campine; Karl Sabourin as Houdan; Rob Herron as Leghorn; Niall Sullivan as Wyandotte; Cenia Monteiro as Ancona; Erin Cleary as Araucana; Meghan O'Donnell as Bandara; Lisa Repetti as Sandy; Melissa Bender as Silkie; Katie Crocker as Buttercup; Jennifer Logan as Catalana; Jada Thirdgill as Lamona; Dennis Murphy as Dorking; Jack Bailey as Frizzle; and Joey Bazinet as Orpington.

Scene 1. [*The chicken coop, just before feeding time. A feed bin sits center. SILKIE, a drama chicken stands d.c. reciting lines from the upcoming play 'Romeo and Juliet'. She is dressed mostly in dark clothing - the kind of fashion that drama kids wear to draw attention to their disdain for attention.*]

SILKIE.   Two fowl groups, both like in dignity, In fair chicken coop, where they lay their eggs, From ancient grudge break to new mutiny, Where deep mistrust makes sparring chicken legs. From forth the hostile flocks of these two foes A pair of star-cross'd pullets try their luck; Whose misadventured piteous thoughts Do with their schemes make their buddies cluck. The fitful passage of their chicken love, And the continuance of their peer groups' rage, Which, but their chicken brains, nought could remove Is now the forty minutes on our stage; The which if you with patient ears attend, What here shall miss, our fowl shall strive to mend.

[*She concludes her speech and produces a dinner bell. Upon hearing her ring it, the other chickens enter from L. (the drama chickens) and R (the football chickens) and rush the feed bin, DC. They segregate by type and begin to "eat" their lunches. Lamona moves left to join her group.*]

SANDY.   Whatcha doin' here so early, Silkie?

SILKIE.   Oh Hi Sandy! I just wanted to practice the prologue sometime today before drama class, so I thought I'd cut out to lunch early.

SANDY.   Good idea. You off book yet?

SILKIE.   Ya! Like that's a problem. I only have like four lines in the whole play.

BUTTERCUP. How about you, Sandy? Are you off book yet?

SANDY.   Well, no. Geez, there are so many lines!

4

CATALANA. Listen honey, anytime you wanna give up Juliet, there's plenty of us that would love a chance at that role!

LAMONA.   Yeah, look out for sharp objects, honey! I could step into that role in a minute!

CATALANA. Well, Lamona, you'd be the first black hen ever to capture Romeo's heart.

LAMONA.   Listen sistah, Romeo's gonna like what Lamona's showing him up on her balcony!!

HENS.   Ow! Ow!! [*They cackle wildly.* DORKING, FRIZZLE *and* ORPINGTON *approach the drama hens.*]

LEGHORN.   Hey Wyandotte, can you help me?

WYANDOTTE.   Sure, Leghorn, what's up?

LEGHORN.   Oh Man? I keep flunking the big sociology exam.

WYANDOTTE.   Leghorn! You take "*soshe*"!? Wow you surprise me.

LEGHORN.   Ya, but it's way over my head.

WYANDOTTE. Now that *doesn't* surprise me.

LEGHORN.   If I don't pass this test, I'll never get into Purdue!

WYANDOTTE. Purdue, huh? That's a big place!

LEGHORN.   You ain't kidding! The recruiter guy said I have what it takes to be a Purdue Roaster! [*strikes a pose.*]

WYANDOTTE. So what kind of help you lookin' for?

LEGHORN.   Just give me the answers on the exam. I got it right here. ·

WYANDOTTE. How did you get hold of the exam already?

LEGHORN.   Oh, I've been taking the same one all year.

WYANDOTTE. Well fire away, Leghorn. What's the first one you have trouble with?

LEGHORN [*looks at paper*] Why did the chicken cross the road?

WYANDOTTE. Well, that's easy... so she could lay it on the line! [*They fade into their group, R.*]

FRIZZLE. Hey Buttercup, what's all the cackling about?

BUTTERCUP. Oh nothing you would understand, at all, Frizzle.

FRIZZLE. Aw c'mon, try me! I know more than you think.

CATALANA. Nah, Frizz, it's just not up your alley. It wouldn't be right.

FRIZZLE. Give me a break, will ya?

LAMONA. Now Dorking here, his strut tells all! [*DORKING preens, struts.*]

HENS. Yes, yes!!

LAMONA. He'd "get it" in a minute!

HENS. Ooooh!!!

FRIZZLE. Hey, I know where eggs come from ... [*They all cackle wildly.*]

CATALANA. OK, Frizz, tell us ... what came first, the chicken or the egg?

[*They cackle again, only this time, their laughter is interrupted by a football that has been tossed into their group by the football players, hitting one of them. Their laughter dissolves into sounds of protest.*]

DORKING. Hey! What's the big idea?

ORPINGTON. Take your brain-dead game somewhere else. This is where we eat.

CAMPINE. Oh gee. Sorry. Ha ha ha!

DORKING. You think that's funny, little capon boy?

DANNY. Who you calling capon boy, Dorkling?

DORKING. That's Dorking. No 'L'.

HOUDAN. Well how'd you like to be a chicken with no "u" after I get through with you?

FRIZZLE. Well actually, Cocky Locky, there's no "u" in Chicken.

HOUDAN. There isn't?

DANNY. No Houdan. No there isn't.

CATALANA. No problem. There's no problem here. I'll just clean this up. [*She scoops up the feed spilled by the football and dumps it over ANCONA'S head.*]

ALL. [*Oooh! Ohh! Cluck! Cluck! etc.*]

HOUDAN. Ya know that's the kind of thing that gets drama chickens annihilated. Not that that's going to happen or anything, but annihilation of chickens could happen.

ORPINGTON. Yeah, well why don't you just bring it on, tough guy?

BUCKEYE. It's no fair fighting drama fairies like you.

ORPINGTON. Try me, egg sucker.

ALL. [*Oooh! Ohh! Cluck! Cluck! etc.*]

BUCKEYE. But who says fights have to be fair?

[*Music. "Turkey in the Straw". DANNY and DORKING commence fighting, BUCKEYE singles out ORPINGTON, CAMPINE and HOUDAN go for FRIZZLE. BUTTERCUP, CATALANA and LAMONA take on the cheerleaders. After a few moments of pitched struggle, Principal PULLET enters. All separate to their sides. Music ceases.*]

ALL. Principal Pullet! Principal Pullet! Pullet is here! Quit it!

PULLET. Rebellious bantams, enemies to peace, Profaners of this chicken coop school, - Will they not hear? What, ho! you birds, you beasts, That quench the fire of your pernicious rage

With vicious pecking issuing from your beaks, On pain of torture, from those bird-brained heads Throw your misguided conflict to the ground, And hear the sentence of your principal. Three civil brawls, bred of an airy word, By thee, old Drama club, and Football team, Have thrice disturb'd the quiet of our coop, If ever you disturb our roosts again, Your necks shall pay the forfeit of the peace. For this time, all the rest depart away. You leading man; shall go along with me. And, quarterback, come you this afternoon, To know our further pleasure in this case. [*The chickens depart, each to their own places.* DORKING *accompanies* PULLET *off*.]

Scene 2. [*Another place in the coop, an hour or so later. The football chickens are hanging out.*]

BUCKEYE.   Wow, that was close.

CAMPINE.   Yeah, we mighta gotten thrown right outa the coop

HOUDAN.   Not cool, Not cool.

BUCKEYE.   We got the big game against Tyson coming up.

CAMPINE.   Well, whattya think is gonna happen to Danny?

HOUDAN.   I dunno - Pullet seemed pretty heated when she was talking to him.

BUCKEYE.   She won't kick him out, he's our quarterback! She'd be crazy to mess with the football team.

CAMPINE.   Yeah, don't you worry, if there's anything around here that's number one on everybody's mind, it's football.

HOUDAN.   Yeah, man! Football is NUMBER ONE!!

BUCKEYE, CAMPINE and HOUDAN. We're number one! We're number one! Squawk, [*etc.*]

CHEERLEADERS. Hey! That's our job!!! We're number one! We're number one! Squawk, [*etc.*]

BUCKEYE. Cool it, cool it chicks, here they come.

LEGHORN. Why did the chicken cross the basketball court?

WYANDOTTE. He heard the referee calling fowls. [*DANNY enters.*]

ANCONA. Hey Danny!

ARAUCANA. Hey Danny!!

BANDARA. Hey Danny!!!

DANNY. Oh, Hi chicks.

BUCKEYE. So, what gives? Huh?

CAMPINE. Yeah, what did Pullet have to say?

HOUDAN. Are you in trouble?

DANNY. Nah, are you kidding me? She just went on and on about bad blood springing from the loins of old partisans and weird crap like that.

HOUDAN. Man, that is WHACK!!

DANNY. Yeah, I'm supposed to like apologize or something like that.

CAMPINE. Oh yeah, right, like you would ever apologize to a drama geek!

HOUDAN. Those chickens that act the way they do might just find themselves with their necks snapped. Not that I'm saying that I would do that, but neck snappage could definitely happen.

CAMPINE. Well, I hear they're having a party tonight.

ANCONA, ARAUCANA, BANDARA. Eewww, drama chicks dancing! Eeeewww!

BUCKEYE. Why would anybody want to go to a drama party?

HOUDAN. I wouldn't be caught dead at one.

WYANDOTTE. Me neither.

CAMPINE. Not me.

DANNY. Well, I was thinking of stopping by…kind of pay them a surprise visit.

CAMPINE. I might go.

WYANDOTTE. Yeah, Iwas thinking of going.

HOUDAN. Me too.

DANNY. That chick Silkie, she's kinda hot – I mean for a Drama geek.

BUCKEYE. Dude - don't even go there! If I ever thought you'd look at a Drama chick, Dude - I'd totally disown you.

DANNY. Well, it would be fun to crash their party.

CAMPINE. Yeah.

HOUDAN. Yeah.

BUCKEYE. Yeah

DANNY. Besides, we might see something good ...

CAMPINE. Yeah.

HOUDAN. Yeah.

BUCKEYE. Yeah

ANCONA. Yeah.

ARAUCANA. Yeah.

BANDARA. Yeah.

LEGHORN. Why did the dinosaur cross the road?

WYANDOTTE.   Because chickens hadn't evolved yet.
[Exeunt.]

Scene 3. [*Later, at another place in the coop. The Drama chickens are partying. "Psycho Chicken" by The Fools is heard loudly as the chickens dance. During the dancing, the football chickens creep into the scene, surrounding the unnoticing Drama chickens. The music abruptly stops.*]

ORPINGTON.   Hey! What the cluck!!
OTHERS.   Hey! What happened to the music, [etc.]
CAMPINE.   Well how can you chickens dance to that stuff?
HOUDAN.   Yeah, that music is lame-o!
CAMPINE.   What's wrong with you Drama geeks anyway?
ANCONA.   That's not real music.
ARAUCANA.   You can't dance to that.
BANDARA.   Your taste is in your beak.
ANCONA.   If this was a real party
ARAUCANA.   With real cool chicks
BANDARA.   Then we'd have real music
ANCONA, ARAUCANA, BANDARA.   That real chicks could dig.
HOUDAN.   Yeah, music like that is totally not poultry like.
I mean chickens that listen to garbage like that could be destroyed or something. Not that I'm saying that that's gonna happen, but total destruction could be brought on if ya know what I mean.

11

BUCKEYE.   Cool it Houdan.

LEGHORN.   Why did the turkey cross the road?

WYANDOTTE.   To prove he wasn't chicken

ANCONA.   Hey Campine, did you bring that CD?

CAMPINE.   Um, yeah. I think. Uh, yeah. Here it is.

ARAUCANA.   Well put it on!

BANDARA.   Yeah let's show these drama geeks and freaks what real dancing is!

CAMPINE.   And real music!

ANCONA, ARAUCANA, BANDARA.   Yeah let's get our groove on!!! [*Campine struggles to work the CD player.*]

BUTTERCUP.   Hey, Having trouble?

CATALANA.   Why don't you try plugging it in?!

CAMPJNE.   Oh crud, look. The cord is loose!

FRIZZLE.   Great move! [*The Music starts and the football chickens all begin enthusiastically dancing to the "Chicken Dance Polka". The drama chickens are not participating, and as they watch, SILKIE moves D.C., DANNY, seeing his chance, slips the dance and moves to intercept her.*]

DANNY.   Hi, ah, it's Silkie, right?

SILKIE.   Yeah.

DANNY.   Yeah, well, ah, I'm Danny, and, ah, I was maybe, ah, maybe just wondering ... Silkie, right? If you, ah ...

SILKIE.   Yes, that's my name.

DANNY.   Yeah! Silkie! I was with the football players over there, and ...

SILKIE.   OH! Yeah! The football players!

DANNY.   The football players!

SILKIE. The guys who are crashing my party!

DANNY. Yeah, um, right, yeah ...

SILKIE. Yeah, so what are you doing here?

DANNY. Oh well I mean ...

SILKIE. Don't you feel just a little out of place?

DANNY. I just ... good music, good music ...

SILKIE. Ya know what? Just tell it to my friend Sandy here, yeah. [*She pulls Sandy between them and fades off, disgusted.*]

DANNY. Sandy?

SANDY. Hi.

DANNY. Wow.

SANDY. Hi.

DANNY. Hi. How ... how ya doing? I'm Da-Danny

SANDY. Danny! I'm Sandy!

DANNY. You're Sandy!

SANDY. Ya!

DANNY. I'm on the football team.

SANDY. I'm in Drama!

DANNY. Oh...wow ...it's really nice to ...meet you.

SANDY. It's really nice to meet you.

DANNY. So anyway, I ...

BUCKEYE. What's going on?!

DANNY. Hey, Buckeye. I was just-

BUCKEYE. She's a loser Drama geek, Danny. Don't talk to her.

ALL. [*React. 'Ohhhh! Cluck! cluck!, cluck!', etc.*]

LAMONA. Whoa, whoa, whoa, whoa!

13

BANDARA.　　Excuse me! Excuse me!

LAMONA.　　Miss Lamona will straighten this right out. You're struttin' the wrong way.

BANDARA.　　Oh, drama chickens are WHACK!

ALL.　　[React. 'Ohhhh! Cluck! cluck!, cluck!', etc.]

LAMONA.　　Your Mama should have fried you at birth!

BANDARA.　　Your mama couldn't lay an egg if her life depended on it!

LAMONA.　　I'd rather be one of my mother's eggs than be a skanky old chicken fricassee, whack eyed, Colonel Sanders twenty-two secret spiced 'ho' like your Mama.

ALL.　　[React. 'Ohhhh! Cluck! cluck!, cluck!', etc.]

BANDARA.　　Your mama is pecked bald AND ugly.

ALL.　　[React. 'Ohhhh! Cluck! cluck!, cluck!', etc.]

LAMONA.　　You don't have a Mama. Your Mama is a Egg-Beater[tm].

ALL.　　[React. 'Ohhhh! Cluck! cluck!, cluck!', etc.]

BANDARA.　　At least I got plumage in the right places unlike you.

LAMONA.　　Oh I look good. [to others] Don't you think I look good?

DRAMA CHICKS.　　Yeah!!

BANDARA.　　Back up ... Back up ...

LAMONA.　　You know what? Why don't you back up?!

BANDARA.　　Oh no!

LAMON A.　　Oh yes, oh yes!

[ORPINGTON runs and kneels behind BANDARA, as LAMONA gives her a vicious shove. BANDARA goes over backwards and the battle is on, chicken style (with music). After a few moments, the chickens begin to *separate and withdraw to each side. The music stops. (Football chickens, R. and Drama Chickens L.) As they go, DANNY and SANDY are the last to leave the stage. They look with longing and sorrow to each other as they are drawn off R. and L. respectively.]*

Scene 4. [*The henhouse. Late at night. Sandy is trying, without any success, to lay an egg.*]

DANNY.　　She squawks! O, squawk again, bright angel, for you are as glorious to this roost, over my head as a winged messenger of heaven to the white-upturned wondering eyes of

mortals that fall back to gaze on him when he bestrides the lazy-pacing clouds and sails upon the bosom of the air! [*Aside.*] Holy cow! Where did that Cheez Whiz[TM] come from?

SANDY.　　Who's there?

DANNY.　　Sandy?

SANDY.　　Danny? What are you doing here?

DANNY.　　I've never been in the hen house before ...

SANDY.　　I'm not decent! Wait a minute!

DANNY.　　WHOA! [*Worried he might spy something he shouldn't, he averts his eyes.*]

SANDY.　　OK!

DANNY.　　Uh, it's me, Danny from the-ah-party tonight.

SANDY.　　Hi Danny.

DANNY.　　Hey. Ah ...I was just wondering ...what are ya ...what are ya doing?

15

SANDY.   Ummm ...right before you walked in I was trying to lay an egg.

DANNY.   Oh ... why?

SANDY.   Well ... I dunno. I guess I'm just supposed to.

DANNY.   Well ... that's cool.

SANDY.   No, it's not really.

DANNY.   It's not? I mean it's not! Right... That's definitely not cool.

SANDY.   Well, I mean, what's the point? Right?

DANNY.   Uh ... yeah. What's the point? [*long pause*] Huh huh. [*he laughs nervously, another pause*] What *is* the point?

SANDY.   Well, reproduction. Every hen lays an egg every day, and the next day, it disappears. The population remains the same no matter what.

DANNY.   Oh, yeah, the population. I see what you mean.

SANDY.   Well, you didn't come all the way over here to talk about laying, did you?

DANNY.   Laying, well, um, um, no. NO! [*She smiles.*]

SANDY.   So what's on your mind?

DANNY.   I was ...was just thinking, you know, about how the Prom is coming, and I haven't really found anybody to go with. Did you find anybody?

SANDY.   Ahh, I wasn't really sure if I was gonna go.

DANNY.   Oh cuz...

SANDY.   It's kinda lame. All those jocks dancing around.

DANNY.   Yeah ...

SANDY.   Lamely ...

DANNY.   Yeah ... there's a lot of them there ... There's not enough other chicks to choose from.

SANDY. Right, right. I'd be ostracized there.

DANNY. I wouldn't ostracize you, cuz ... I'm cool like that.

SANDY. Oh you are?

DANNY. Yeah, I'm more eclectic than my friends suspect.

SANDY. Eclectic!

DANNY. Well, not really. That's one of my vocab words I'm supposed to use in a sentence this week ...

SANDY. You didn't really come up here to practice your vocab list either, did you? 'Cuz it's gettin' kinda late ...

DANNY. Yeah ... sorry ... ummm ...

SANDY. Why are you here in the middle of the night?

DANNY. I was just thinking you know, cuz you know Silkie and all ... I was thinking of asking her but ...

SANDY. Yes ...

DANNY. Then I saw you. [*empty pause*] and I was like - she looks like a really cool chick ... maybe I could take that cool chick to the Prom and...

SANDY. You think I'm a cool chick?

DANNY. Yeah ...

SANDY. And you wanna go to the prom with me?

DANNY. Well, yeah.

SANDY. What about your cheerleader chicks that follow you around?

DANNY. Oh those cheep chicks? Naw. Ever since I saw you at the party, my whole world changed.

SANDY. But your friends ...

DANNY. Love can do whatever love dares to do ...

SANDY. Love?

17

DANNY. Love.

SANDY. Oh Danny!

DANNY. Oh Sandy!

SANDY. Let's go to the prom together. We can throw caution to the wind!

DANNY. Great! Listen, it's almost morning. I've got to get back.

SANDY. Will I see you again soon?

DANNY. I'll try to see you tomorrow.

[*They start to separate, then kiss tenuously before exiting.*]

Scene 5. [*The next day, at the rehearsal of 'Romeo and Juliet'.*]

BUTTERCUP. Alright, drama chickens please find your positions onstage. We're rehearsing the swordfight scene. Romeo Mercutio and Tybalt onstage please ... [*The actors mentioned take their places.*] ... alright, and ... GO!

FRIZZLE. O calm, dishonorable, vile submission! Alla stoccata carries it away. [*Gets in ORPINGTON'S face.*] Tybalt, you rat-catcher, will you walk?

ORPINGTON. [*Not backing away.*] What wouldst thou have with me?

FRIZZLE. Good king of cats, nothing but one of your nine lives; that I mean to make bold withal, and as you shall use me hereafter, drybeat the rest of the eight. Will you pluck your beak out? Make haste, lest mine be about your ears beforehand.

ORPINGTON. I am for you. [*Grabs FRIZZLE.*]

DORKING Gentle Mercutio, put thy beak up.

FRIZZLE. Come, sir, your passado. [*They fight.*]

DORKING. Come, Benvolio; beat down their weapons. Gentlemen, for shame, forbear this outrage! [*Steps between ORPINGTON. And FRIZZLE.*] Tybalt, Mercutio, the prince expressly hath forbidden bandying in Verona streets. Hold, Tybalt! good Mercutio! [*ORPINGTON pecks FRIZZLE under DORKING'S arm.*]

FRIZZLE. [*Laying down on the stage, crossing legs.*] I am hurt. A plague o' both your houses! I am sped. Is he gone, and hath nothing?

DORKING What, art thou hurt?

FRIZZLE. Ay, ay, a scratch, a scratch; marry, 'tis enough. Go fetch a surgeon.

DORKING Courage, man; the hurt cannot be much.

FRIZZLE. No, 'tis not so deep as a well, nor so wide as a church-door; but 'tis enough, 'twill serve. ask for me to-morrow, and you shall find me a grave man.

[*During this action, the female drama chickens who are watching become more and more distressed with the need to go to the bathroom.*]

BUTTERCUP.　　　OK, Potty Parade! ! Five minute break!

OTHERS.　　Oh Boy!, Yippee!, Cluck, Squawk, [*FRIZZLE and the hens exit. DORKING and ORPINGTON move left.*]

DORKING.　　Hey how about that party last night at Silkie's.

ORPINGTON.　　　Oh yeah.

DORKING.　　lt was going great until those football freaks showed up.

ORPINGTON.　　　Who told them they could come out after dark anyway. Wusses. [*During this, DANNY, BUCKEYE, and HOUDAN steal in and stand behind DORKING and ORPINGTON.*]

19

DORKING. Yeah, I'd really like to kick that Danny's tail just for breathing.

ORPINGTON . Hey, did you see the way he was trying to get his freak on with Silkie.

DORKING. Never mind that. How about the way he was looking at Sandy!

ORPINGTON. Yeah. If I see him with her at all, I'll pluck him bald.

DORKING. He'll be Pot Pie when I'm done with him.

ORPINGTON. Yeah and that moron Buckeye. Someone needs to cluck him up! [*SANDY enters L.*]

SANDY. Danny! Wh-what are you doing here?

DANNY. Sandy, we were just...

BUCKEYE. We were thinking of joining the drama club, but...

DANNY. We were just checking things out.

HOUDAN. Drama geeks like you totally give poultry like a bad image. I mean chickens that prance around and talk like that could be smashed to chunks or something. Not that I'm saying that that's gonna happen, but total chunkage could be brought on if ya know what I mean.

BUCKEYE. But on second thought we have a measure of self respect, which is more than you pathetic poultry can say for your sorry selves.

DORKING. I'll show you pathetic you gutless capon. [*ORPINGTON holds him back.*]

DANNY. C'mon, try me.

DORKING. Bring it on.

SANDY. Danny, don't!

DORKING. Let's go, Mr. Football Hero!

DANNY. I don't want to mess you up.

SANDY. Danny, leave him alone.

BUCKEYE. Since when do you take orders from that pathetic creep?

DORKING. Let's go Mr. Big Stuff!

DANNY. Nah, some other time, HATCHLING!

DORKING. Oh, too chicken, huh?

BUCKEYE. Hey, he's not chicken! If he wanted to rip your head off, he could do it anytime.

DORKING You stow it, Dipstick.

BUCKEYE. Here' s your dipstick! [*He begins to attack DORKING. Combat ensues, with music, and BUCKEYE ends up badly beaten on the floor. The action should always be more pantomimed and humorous than strongly dramatic. As BUCKEYE falls, the COMPANY enters to watch.*]

DANNY. Now, Dorking, take the medicine you give, That you just gave to Buckeye lying there He soon will be in the infirmary, And you may go to keep him company. Either you; or I, or both, must go with him.

DORKING. You, wretched punk, that did escort him here,

you can go with him to infirmary.

DANNY. We'll see about that. [*They fight. DORKING falls. At the same time, Principal PULLET enters. All grow silent.*]

PULLET. Danny beat him, he laid poor Buckeye low; Who now the price of his safety doth owe? For this offence, young Danny is exiled Beyond the coop, behind the guano pile. No football games for you, son, not for you, Not Tyson, Colonel Sanders or Purdue Your teammates will have suffered to be sure- While you live out your days beyond manure. If I so much as see you at the prom, I'll pluck you of your feathers and your comb. When graduation comes in its own time, Then you will sure regret these words of mine. I will be deaf to pleading and excuses; Nor tears nor prayers shall purchase out abuses. Therefore use none. let Danny get himself beyond the gate And way beyond the crap pile wait and wait.

[Friends drag the beaten chickens offstage. Danny and Sandy kiss passionately before separating.]

Scene 6. *[BUTTERCUP, BANDARA, CATALANA, and LEGHORN & WYANDOITE each take their place in separate spots across the front of the stage to address the audience. They are lit one at a time.]*

BUTTERCUP. Now Dorking has been beaten by the foe And has been carted off his crown to mend. He can no longer play fair Romeo, But gives that juicy role o'er to his friend. Yet Frizzle is himself too much a wimp. His mannerisms too much like a hen; His voice too sweet; his swordplay way too limp. The drama club, alas too short of men; But yet, there being no one else to play The role, it's passed along to Master Frizzle. He can't recall the words that he must say - His brainstorms always seem more like a drizzle.

BANDARA. The Principal, Miss Pullet, so it seems – Though charged with educating bantam minds - Has less regard for football in her schemes, But casts disdain, instead, on athlete kinds. The football team itself is in a fix With Buckeye out. Their hope of winning wanes With Danny gone to live among the sticks, And eke his meager living on the plains. So Wyandotte is calling signals now. He lobbed a pass to Houdan o'er the fence,

And Houdan, he got stepped on by a cow – A taste for him of his own cruel intents.

CATALANA. Our star-crossed pullets yearn to find a way To have their corn, and yet, to eat it too. For them, forbidden fruits are plucked each day, And first-time love creates each bird anew.

But Sandy has a plan, and don't you know When daily strutting takes her past the stile She smuggles out the script for Romeo,

And in between each kiss and sacch'rine smile She's teaching Danny all about the Bard. They practice every line and every scene In hopes that he may come back to the yard And be her valiant King and she his Queen.

LEGHORN. Why did the chicken cross the road, roll in the mud and cross the road again?

WYANDOTTE.   Because he was a dirty double-crosser.

Scene 7. [*One day, outside the chicken coop.*]

SANDY.   Farewell! God knows when we shall meet again. I have a faint cold fear thrills through my veins, That almost freezes up the heat of life. How if, when I am laid into the tomb, I wake before the time that Romeo Come to redeem me? there's a fearful point! Shall I not, then, be stifled in the vault, To whose foul mouth no healthsome air breathes in, And there die strangled ere my Romeo comes? So early waking, what with loathsome smells, And shrieks like mandrakes' torn out of the earth, That living mortals, hearing them, run mad. - O, if I wake, shall I not be distraught? Romeo, I come! this do I drink to thee. [*Drinks. Faints.*]

DANNY.   In faith, I will. Let me peruse this face. For here lies Juliet, and her beauty makes This vault a feasting presence full of light. [*PULLET and the OTHERS silently enter and stand just outside the light, watching this rehearsal.*] O, here Will I set up my everlasting rest, And shake the yoke of inauspicious stars From this world-wearied flesh. Eyes, look your last! Arms, take your last embrace! and, lips, O you The doors of breath, seal with a righteous kiss A dateless bargain to engrossing death! Here's to my love! [*Drinks*] O true apothecary! Thy drugs are quick. Thus with a kiss I die.[*Dies.*]

[*There is a pause. PULLET begins the applause, joined by the OTHERS. DANNY and SANDY sit up, embracing each other.*]

PULLET.   This is what you call banishment?

DANNY.   Yes, Miss Pullet.

SANDY.   Yes, Miss Pullet.

PULLET.   A picnic lunch and an afternoon in the arms of your lover? Hardly what I call punishment!

DANNY.   No Miss Pullet.

SANDY.   No Miss Pullet.

ANCONA.   No Miss Pullet.

ARAUCANA. No Miss Pullet.

BANDARA.   No Miss Pullet.

PULLET.   Shut up! I wasn't talking to you!

ANCONA.   Yes, Miss Pullet.

ARAUCANA. Yes, Miss Pullet.

BANDARA.   Yes, Miss Pullet [*Her glare stops the chatter.*]

PULLET.   Danny, aren't you a little out of your element? This is hardly football X's and O's.

DANNY.   Well, Miss Pullet, we're in love and love does whatever love dares to do ...

PULLET.   Yes, yes, I've read the play too.

SANDY. Well, our love is real, Miss Pullet. No matter what you or anybody else may think. Love is stronger than chicken wire and manure piles. Love can conquer anything.

DANNY. Love is greater than our need to fear each other because we are different. Love has the power to overcome our own self-imposed limitations. And love is stronger than the authority of someone who has forgotten what true love really is.

[*All respond 'Ooooh! Cluck, cluck, cluck' etc.*]

PULLET. [*Pause.*] Well, Danny, Sandy, I suppose a new edict is in order here.

SANDY. Yes, Miss Pullet.

DANNY. Yes, Miss Pullet.

ANCONA. Yes, Miss Pullet.

ARAUCANA. Yes, Miss Pullet.

BANDARA. Yes, Miss Pullet.

PULLET. [*to DANNY and SANDY.*] You are hereby reinstated to the Chicken Coop, and you are sentenced to star in Romeo and Juliet. [*to ALL.*] A loving peace this morning with it brings; The sun, in joy will brightly shine instead. Go hence, to have more talk of these 'love' things; Some shall be pardon' d, and some punish-ed. There never was a story of more woe Than that of Juliet and her Romeo.

LEGHORN .[*to WYANDOTTE*] Why did the turtle cross the road?

PULLET. Oh for Gosh sakes, Leghorn, to get to the shell station!

[*Exeunt.*]   *Finis.*]

Other Plays by Don Bliss,

available from Sugarhouse Press

Tears of St. Lucy

Drama. 1 Act. Paperback. 39 Pages. $10.00.

Beneath the streets of Boston, a story unfolds of ambition, vanity, faith and the incorrigible nature of humanity. Martin and Mary Doul, both blind, are two of the many street people who take shelter in the Blue Line of the MBTA. When Cardinal Lowe comes into the possession of a valuable relic unearthed by Boston's "big dig", he sees his opportunity to restore the church's tarnished image while changing the lives of the unwitting couple forever. A modern day retelling of John Synge's "The Well of the Saints." 4m, 4w plus extras. 1 int.

Voices from September 11th

Drama. By Don Bliss, Bill Comeau, Paperback. 66 Pages. $11.99

Arising from the initial pain, anguish, fear, and hopelessness, young voices rise together to articulate the youthful consciousness of the watershed event of the 21st century. Written for and developed by high school actors in Massachusetts and Rhode Island, "Voices from September 11th" presents the clear, candid and indomitable spirit of America's youth in the face of her greatest modern tragedy. May be performed as full length, assembly length or as monologues. 4-10m/5-17w, multiple interiors and exteriors.

The Power of Darkness

Drama. 1 Act. Paperback. 43 Pages. $10.00

Banned in Russia for decades after its writing, Tolstoy's "The Power of Darkness" is the product of an age of political violence and the search for personal responsibility. Nikita seduces a young and vulnerable Marinka and then marries Anisiya, who has murdered her husband. Soon tired of her, he impregnates her daughter, and then conspires to murder the baby. The entire household is drawn deeper into the darkness of sin and depravity until the inevitable climax. Adapted to an assembly length one act, this piece makes for stirring drama in the constructivist classroom. 9m, 8w plus extras, singers. 1 Int., 1 Ext.

<u>Mikado Enterprises, L.L.C.</u>

Comedy. Full length. Libretto. Paperback. 70 Pages. $9.00.

Executions have been traded for terminations in this rollicking update of the Gilbert and Sullivan classic. Katisha is now the elderly cleaning lady, while the hapless Koko is the Vice President of Human Resources who must terminate anyone involved in an office romance - including himself! Along comes Nanki-poo, the IPS delivery driver who is adored by the "three little girls from the (secretarial) pool!" See them all scramble when the CEO springs a surprise visit to the Boardroom!

4-5m/4-5w, plus male and female chorus. Area staging.

<u>Dickens' A Christmas Carol</u>

Drama. Three Acts. Paperback. 64 Pages. $8.00.

Charles Dickens' timeless classic re-adapted for the modern high school theater. This script brings the audience once again into the cold and dark rooms of Ebenezer Scrooge that, like his heart, will be transformed by a succession of spectral visits.

16m/14w/15 flex. Area Staging.

www.sugarhousepress.com

Don Bliss, in addition to writing, directed high school theater for twenty-two years before retiring, and now serves full-time as a Congregational Pastor in southeastern Massachusetts. He has worked as an Artist in Residence in the public schools. As an actor, he has performed in both professional and amateur settings on Cape Cod and in New York, and throughout the US.